젓가락여자

아시아에서는 《바이링궐 에디션 한국 대표 소설》을 기획하여 한국의 우수한 문학을 주제별로 엄선해 국내외 독자들에게 소개합니다. 이 기획은 국내외 우수한 번역가들이 참여하여 원작의 품격을 최대한 살렸습니다. 문학을 통해 아시아의 정체성과 가치를 살피는 데 주력해 온 아시아는 한국인의 삶을 넓고 깊게 이해하는 데 이 기획이 기여하기를 기대합니다.

Asia Publishers presents some of the very best modern Korean literature to readers worldwide through its new Korean literature series 〈Bilingual Edition Modern Korean Literature〉. We are proud and happy to offer it in the most authoritative translation by renowned translators of Korean literature. We hope that this series helps to build solid bridges between citizens of the world and Koreans through a rich in-depth understanding of Korea.

바이링궐 에디션 한국 대표 소설 074

Bi-lingual Edition Modern Korean Literature 074

Chopstick Woman

천운영
젓가락여자

Cheon Un-yeong

ASIA
PUBLISHERS

Contents

젓가락여자

Chopstick Woman

제가 부탁해볼게요. 어떻게는요. 직접 만나서 물어보
죠 뭐. 우리 독서토론회에 와줄 수 있냐고. 왜 못 만나
요? 약속도 되어 있는데. 내일이요. 저녁 먹기로 했어
요. 저 서진 작가 잘 알아요. 학교 후배예요. 그냥 좀 아
는 게 아니구. 친했어요. 자취도 같이 했는걸. 친했으니
까 방도 같이 썼죠. 왜 여태 말 안 했느냐고요? 누가 물
어봤어야 말을 하죠. 물어보지도 않은 걸 굳이 말할 필
요도 없는 거고. 누구 좀 압네, 하는 거 유치하잖아요.
유명한 사람 이름 들먹이면서 자기도 대단한 사람이라
고 착각하는, 그걸 뭐라 그러더라? 퍼스트네임클럽? 저

I'll ask her. How? Well, I'll just see her in person and ask. I'll just ask her if she could come to our reading club meeting. Why not? I've already made an appointment with her. Tomorrow. We'll have dinner together. I know So Jin very well. We went to the same university, me being junior to her. We're not just on nodding terms. We were close. Room-mates. Close enough to share a room. Why haven't I told you about it? Well, you've never asked. So, I haven't felt the need to bring it up. Boasting that you know some famous person—isn't that a little childish? You know those people, who feel as if mentioning some celebrity's name makes them

그런 사람 아니거든요? 어쨌든 이달의 작가 독서토론 다 끝내고, 마지막 주에 작가초청강연 듣는 거, 정말 좋은 아이디어예요. 이번 기회에 아예 정례화해도 좋겠어요. 초청강연이 너무 거창하면 그냥 작가와의 만남 정도로. 우리 발표한 거 정리해서 자료집도 만들고. 기념으로 작가한테 선물도 하고.

아이 참, 진짜라니까요. 금방 들통 날 거짓말을 왜 해요. 뭐 얻어먹을 게 있다구. 글쎄요. 아마 단칼에 자르지는 못할 거예요. 저한테 빚진 게 좀 있거든요. 금전적으로 그렇다는 게 아니라, 아무튼 그런 게 있어요. 다른 사람은 몰라도 제 부탁은 거절 못할 거예요. 나쁜 일도 아니고. 독자와의 만남인데. 언니 일정이 어떨지 몰라서 장담은 못하겠지만. 그래도 일단 말은 건네볼게요. 학교 다닐 때요? 단정적으로 뭐라 말하긴 어렵지만……그럼 언니 처음 만났을 때 얘기 해드릴까요? 얘기가 길텐데. 이따가 독회 끝나고 하면 안 되나? 알았어요, 지금 할게요. 아, 진짜 오래전 일이다. 그런데 어쩌면 이렇게 생생하게 다 기억나지?

somebody, too. What do you call them? A member of the First Name Club? I'm not that kind of person, you see. Anyhow, it's a brilliant idea to schedule the guest writer's lecture for the final week, after the Read and Discuss the Writer of the Month sessions are all over. I prefer to make it a regular practice. If Guest Writer Lecture sounds much too grand, let's call it something like a "Meet the Writer." We can collect and edit our presentations into a book. And we can also give souvenirs to the writers, perhaps?

Yes, it's true. I'm telling you. Why would I tell a lie that you could find out in no time? What would I gain by lying? Well, I don't think she'll flat out refuse. She owes me one. Not money, though.

Anyway, there's something like that between us. She may be able to refuse someone else's request, but not mine. We're not proposing any shady deals here. It's just a meeting with her readers. I don't know her schedule, so I can't guarantee it. But, I'll at least talk to her about it. Her university years? It's hard to give you a summary answer... Well, should I tell you how I met her for the first time? It's a long story, though. Can't we do it after the reading session? Okay then, I'll tell you now. Ah, it's been

그러니까 거기가 학교 앞 술집이었어요. 지하민속주점. 환기시설이 좋지 않았죠. 그 자욱한 담배 연기. 누구 생일파티 겸 개강총회 뒤풀이였는데. 돌아가며 한 가락씩 노래도 부르고, 흩어졌다가 모였다가, 한쪽에서는 울고 또 한쪽에서는 싸우고. 난 뭐 술도 잘 못하고 그런게 다 시시하기도 하고. 그래서 그냥 술이나 홀짝이면서 사람들 지켜봤지. 내 옆에 앉은 동기애는 뒤늦게 과가 어쩌니 적성이 어쩌니 미래가 어쩌니 늘어놓고 있고. 나는 고개만 끄덕끄덕하면서 언제 빠져나가나 하고 둘러보는데, 그때 내 앞에 한 여자가 눈에 딱 들어오는거야. 머리를 길게 늘어뜨리고 앉아 있는데, 가만히 보니까 젓가락 끝으로 김칫국물을 찍어가지고 식탁 위에다가 뭔가 열심히 그리고 있어요. 김칫국 놀이가 자기에게 주어진 임무인 것처럼. 그 일을 묵묵히 수행하고 있는 사람처럼. 그런데 이 여자가 갑자기 고개를 쳐들고 젓가락으로 식탁을 탁 치면서 외치는 거야.

깃발을 꽂아, 깃발을!

딱 이 목소리였어요. 약간 보이시한, 늙은 여가수 같은, 그릉그릉한 목소리. 한 백 년쯤 줄창 담배만 피우고

ages. Then again, somehow, I still remember those times so clearly!

Let me see... It was in a pub in front of the university. A basement pub. With bad ventilation. Filled with cigarette smoke. It was somebody's birthday party/new semester general assembly after-party. We were singing in turn. Some mingling. Others still crying in the corners or fighting one another. As for me, I wasn't much of a drinker and I wasn't too interested in anything that was going on there. So, I just sat at a table sipping my drink, watching everyone around me. One girl, the same year as me, was complaining about having chosen the wrong field against her true aptitude and prospects, blah blah blah. I nodded halfheartedly every now and then, just waiting for a chance to escape the situation.

But then, a woman sitting across from me caught my eye. She had long hair covering her bowed face. She dipped the tip of a chopstick in the kimchi juice and suddenly began to draw something on the table in earnest. As if that were a task assigned to her. Then, she suddenly flung her head upwards and began to yell, slamming the chop-

나면 그런 목소리가 나올까? 아무튼 이게 은근 사람 휘어잡는 목소린데. 그 목소리로 깃발을 꽂으라는 거야. 갑자기 웬 깃발? 뭔 말인가 싶어서 내가 이렇게 쳐다보는데, 이 여자가 젓가락을 입술로 쭉 한번 빨고는 뭉개진 케이크 조각에 푹 꽂아 넣는 거야. 신기하게도 이 젓가락이 안 넘어지고 그대로 서 있어. 다 뭉개진 케이큰데. 그래서 젓가락이 쓰러지나 안 쓰러지나 보고 있는데, 이 여자가 또 그 그릉그릉한 목소리로 말하는 거야.

지금으로부터 십 년 후에다가. 깃대를. 세우란 말야.

그래서 내가 물어봤지.

목표를 가지라구요? 얘는 지금 그게 없어서 문제라는 건데요?

그 여자가 나를 히뜩 올려봐요. 넌 뭐냐, 하는 표정인데 눈빛이 아주 형형해. 그래서 좀 주눅이 들긴 했지만 그래도 눈 똑바로 쳐들고 봤지. 옆에 동기애는 어느새 김치찌개에 머리칼을 담그고 졸고 앉았고.

맞아요. 그 여자가 바로 영은 언니예요. 영은 언니요. 아, 맞다. 서진 작가요. 왜 이렇게 서진이라는 이름이 입에 안 붙지? 그게 본명이에요. 양,영,은. 왜요? 난 더 정

stick on the table.

Raise the flagpole. Run up the flag!

Her voice sounded a bit boyish, or like an old singer's, rattling in her throat. Like the voice of a someone who'd been chain-smoking for about a hundred years. It was a voice capable of making people unwittingly place themselves at her beck and call. Anyways, with that voice, she commanded someone, anyone to raise a flag. What flagpole, what flag? I stared at her, trying to get a sense of what she was talking about. And then, this woman, she took one long suck of the tip of the chopstick, and plunged it into the crumbling piece of cake on the plate in front of her. Oddly, the chopstick didn't fall and remained upright. There was nothing that could support the chopstick upright in that crumbling cake. While I kept my eye on it to see if the chopstick would collapse or not, this woman ordered once more in that thick voice.

Erect. The flagpole. Put it where it'll stay ten years from now.

So, I asked her.

What. You mean we have to have a goal? This girl here, her problem is exactly that. She doesn't have a goal, you see?

감 있고 좋은데. 이보다 이응이 많이 들어간 이름은 들어본 적이 없어. 그런데 성까지 바꿔버릴 줄은 몰랐지. 어쨌거나. 영은 언니가 학교 다닐 때 목소리로 한 카리스마 했죠. 어디 목소리뿐이겠어요? 그 위풍당당한 체격하며. 번득이는 눈빛하며. 옛날엔 지금보다 살집이 좀더 있었거든. 좀이 아니라 꽤 있었지.

아무튼 이 언니가 나를 보고는 씩 웃는 거야. 그러곤 나한테 몸을 바싹 기대고 은근한 목소리로 말하는 거예요.

목표는 없어도 돼. 이 깃발에는 아무것도 씌어져 있지 않거든. 목표 없는 깃발이란 말이지. 십 년 동안은 유예기간이야. 아직 아무것도 쓰지 않아도 되는 기간. 맘껏 즐기고 맘껏 실패하고 맘껏 궁리해도 되는 기간. 어차피 유예기간이니까 상관없잖아. 내가 뭘 하고 싶은지 그때까지만 알아내면 되는 거야. 알아냈으면 그때 가서 깃발에다 쓰는 거지. 나는 가수가 되고 싶다, 엄마가 되고 싶다, 소주가 되고 싶다.

여기까지 말한 언니가 어디서 병뚜껑 하나를 찾아 오더니 젓가락 끝에 올려놔요. 깃발을 매다는 것처럼. 그

The woman stared up at me. What the heck was this? That's what her eyes said. I felt a little timid at first, but kept staring back at her. The girl sitting beside me was now dozing off, a tuft of her hair dipped in a pot of kimchi stew.

Yes, you've guessed it. That woman was none other than Yong-un. Sister Yong-un. Ah—I mean the writer So Jin. I don't know why the name So Jin is so unfamiliar to me. That's her real name. Yang Yong-un.

Why use Yong-un, then? I like her real name better; it has a friendly ring in it. I've never heard of any name with more *i-eung* in it than this one. It had never occurred to me that she would even change her family name. Anyway.

Yong-un was known for her charismatic voice. And her voice wasn't the only thing that drew you to her. Her fine, stately physique. Her piercing eyes. She was a bit on the plump side back then. In fact, much more plump than she is now.

Anyway, this woman gave me a big smile. Then she leaned in close to me and told me, under her breath, as if she were telling me a secret:

You don't need a goal. It's a blank flag; there's nothing on it. I mean, it's an agenda-less flag. You've

리고 병뚜껑을 올린 젓가락을 조심스럽게 뽑아서 빈 소
주병으로 옮겨놓는 거야. 그리고 또 말을 하죠.

자, 이제 이 깃발을, 여기, 십 년 후에다가 옮겨놨어.
여기서부터는 하고 싶은 걸 되게 만드는 유예기간이야.
십 년 잘 놀았으니 또 십 년 아무 생각 없이 달려보는
것도 괜찮잖아? 얼마나 재밌겠어. 하고 싶은 걸 하는데.
열나 노래하고 열나 섹스하고 열나 취하고. 그러다 보
면 가수도 되고 엄마도 되고……

그때 가서 이게 아니다 싶으면요? 되고 싶은 게 안 되
면요?

내가 끼어들며 물었죠. 그랬더니 언니가 또 픽 웃으며
말해요.

뭐가 걱정이야? 다시 꽂으면 되지? 이번엔 진짜진짜
하고 싶은 게 뭔지 알아내면 되잖아. 뭔가 안 되더라도
하고 싶은 걸 했으니 후회는 없을 거 아냐. 안 그래? 깃
발이 여기 있어. 그리고 너는 지금 빈 깃발의 십 년 중
여기 서 있는 거구. 나는 여기쯤? 어이구 나보다 이만큼
이나 더 놀 수 있겠네? 좋겠네?

언니는 팔짱을 낀 채 병을 내려다봐요. 그래서 나도

got a ten-year grace period. You don't need to write anything on it during this time. You can enjoy life to your heart's content. You can fail and make new plans and start all over again. Nothing matters since it's a grace period. All you have to do is figure out what you want to do by the end of the decade. Once you've figured it out, you write it on the flag. I want to be a singer. Or, I want to be a mother. Or, I want to be *soju*.

When she finished talking, she left the table and came back shortly with a bottle cap. Then, she hung it on the tip of her chopstick. As if she were tying a flag to a flagpole. She removed the chopstick from the cake carefully so as not to drop the bottle cap, and then placed it inside an empty *soju* bottle. Then she opened her mouth again.

Now, I've just moved the flag here. Now, it's ten years later. Here, you'll have a different kind of reprieve. Now you have to try to achieve your goal. You've enjoyed yourself for a decade, now it seems fair to go for your goal wholeheartedly, doesn't it? Think about how much fun that'll be! After all, you'll be doing what you really want to do. Singing in earnest, making love in earnest, getting drunk in earnest. Then one day, you'll finally be a

병을 가만히 내려다보았지요. 탁자 저쪽 끝에는 젓가락을 꽂은 소주병이, 탁자 이쪽 끝에는 초록색 라이터가, 그리고 그 사이에는 술이 반쯤 찬 잔이 있어요. 라이터와 술잔의 거리는 반 뼘. 언니와 내 거리가 딱 그만큼이었어요. 나는 언니 병뚜껑에 뭐가 씌어져 있는지 궁금했죠. 그래서 물어봤죠. 언니 깃발에는 뭔가 그려져 있냐고. 그랬더니 아직 아무것도 못 그렸다고 하는 거야. 좀 쓸쓸한 목소리로. 그래서 내가 라이터를 술잔 옆에 나란히 놓으면서 말했죠.

그럼 내 깃발은 여기다가 옮길래요. 난 육 년만 유예 기간을 가져야지? 육 년만 알아보고, 되게 만드는 기간을 이만큼 더 늘려야지? 그럼 내가 언니보다 덜 놀게 되네? 좋겠네요? 나보다 더 많이 노는 거니까? 그런데 열나 취하면 진짜 소주가 될까요?

그때 내 나이 스무 살, 이제 막 대학에 들어온 신입생이었죠. 언니는 스물세 살, 졸업을 앞둔 관록의 여전사였구. 사 년의 사이. 지금이야 같이 늙어가는 처지에 사

20

singer. Or a mother. Or...

But what if, after all that, I realize I've made the wrong choice? Or, I fail to achieve my goal?

I interrupted her with my question. She gave another quick smile and said:

No problem! Then, you just bring the flag back to where it used to be and start all over again. And this time, you make sure that you find out what you really, really want to do. Even if things turn out poorly in the end, you'll have no regrets since you've at least tried to realize your heart's desire. Right? The flag's here. And now, you're standing right here, only this much into the decade of an empty flag. I'm probably around—*here*! You've got a lot longer time left to play than me! Good for you!

She stared down at the bottle and folded her arms. So, I looked down at the bottle silently, too. On the far end of the table was the *soju* bottle with the chopstick stuck in it. On this end of the table was a green lighter. In between there was a half-filled glass of *soju*. The distance between the lighter and the glass was half a span. There was just about the same distance between her and me. I wondered what was written on her bottle cap. So, I asked her. What was on her flag? She answered

년 뭐 대단해요? 하지만 대학에서의 사 년은 정말 아득하잖아요. 군대에서 이등병하고 말년 병장 사이처럼. 언니는 그야말로 저기 먼 하늘에서 힘차게 펄럭이는 깃발이었던 거지. 그런데 여기 땅바닥으로 이제 막 기어올라온 내가, 겁도 없이, 그 아득한 깃발을, 붙잡고 늘어졌으니. 간이 배 밖으로 나온 거지. 그런데 언니는 오히려 그게 맘에 들었나 봐. 그때부터 나 무지하게 챙겨줬잖아. 어디든지 데리고 다니고.

그러니까 그날 그 술집에서 우리는 서로 뭔가 통하고 있다는 걸 느꼈던 거지. 선수가 선수를 알아보는 것처럼. 언니는 나를 찍고, 나는 언니를 찍고. 그런 거 알죠? 전기가 통하는 거. 정말 전기가 짜릿하게 올라오는 기분이었다니까요. 우리는 그렇게 서로를 바라보고 있었죠.

한참 동안을.

그래요, 그때 우린, 뭔가 통했죠. 그래요. 통했어요.

그런데 진짜 중요한 건 바로 지금부터예요. 어느 순간 언니가 허리를 쭉 펴고 기지개를 켜더니, 라이터 옆에 있는 술잔을 집어서 내 앞에 턱하고 내려놓는 거야. 이

she hadn't written anything on it yet. She said this in a little sad voice. So, I picked up the lighter and put it down beside the glass and said:

In that case, I'd like to move my flag to this spot here. I'll only take a six-year grace period. Then I can take longer time to realize my dream. Now, I've less time left to play than you, haven't I? Good for you! You can play longer than me. By the way, if I get dead drunk, will I really turn into *soju*?

I was twenty then. A freshman. She was twenty-three. An experienced woman warrior facing her graduation. Only a four-year difference between us. Now, we're practically getting old side by side, so four years is nothing, really. But at university, four years was a great deal. It's like the distance between a private and a sergeant in the last year of an army service. She was literally a flag soaring high up in the sky. Then I, who'd just climbed up to the surface of the earth undaunted, dared to challenge that flag in the sky. I must have been out of my mind. But then, she seemed to like me the way I was. Because she began to take such good care of me, you see. She took me along with her wherever she went.

제부터 술 좀 마셔볼까? 내가 술이 되나 술이 내가 되나. 너랑 나랑 중에 누가 먼저 술이 되나 한번 보자. 그러더니 순식간에 젓가락을 뽑아 드는 거예요. 칼을 뽑는 사람처럼 쉭. 네, 아까 술병에 꽂아놓았던 그 젓가락이요, 그걸 이렇게 입에 물고는 양손으로 머리를 틀어 올리고, 다시 젓가락을 빼서 머리다발 사이에 푹 꽂는 거야. 이렇게요. 보세요오. 젓가락을 입에 문 다음, 아, 젓가락이 있어야 실감이 나는데 일단 연필로, 머리를 싹 쓸어 모아서, 왼손으로 머리다발 고리를 만들어놓고, 젓가락을 빼서 고리에 집어넣고, 빼고, 이렇게 마무리를 하면! 어때요? 비녀 같지요? X자로 하나 더 꽂을 수도 있어요. 이 과정이 정말 순식간에 이뤄졌다니까요. 휘리릭.

맞아요, 그게 영은 언니 술버릇이에요. 언니 말마따나 술 좀 먹자 싶으면 머리에 젓가락부터 꽂는다니까? 꼭 젓가락이 아니어도 상관없어요. 볼펜이든 칫솔이든 아무튼 뭐든 꽂아서 머리를 틀어 올리고 봐요. 술이요? 진짜 말술이죠. 해 뜨기 전에 끝내질 않아요. 저렇게 마시다가 진짜 술이 되겠다 싶을 정도로. 지금도 그렇게 마

I mean, on that day, we felt like kindred spirits. Just like a pro recognizes a pro. She'd picked me out and I'd picked her out. I felt as if an electric current ran between us. You know what I mean? I really felt something like a tingling sensation of electricity speeding through my body. We kept staring at each other.

For a long while.

Yes, at that time, each of us had some kind of profound understanding of the other. Yes. We both felt it.

Having said that, the most amazing part of the story's yet to come. Suddenly, she straightened her back and took a good long stretch, and then picked up the glass next to the lighter and put it down before me. Shall we go on a spree? We'll see if I turn into *soju* or *soju* turns into me. Let's see which one of us will turn into *soju* first. Then she whipped the chopstick out of the bottle. Like a person drawing a sword. Yes, that very chopstick she'd stuck in the bottle before. She held it between her teeth and then twisted her hair up. Next, she took the chopstick out of her mouth and stuck it into the bunch of her hair. Like this. Look! She put the chopstick between her teeth. Oh, I need a

시려나? 나이가 있어서 안 될 거야. 그땐 젊었으니까. 아무튼 농활 갔을 때 거기 농촌 총각들이 뭣도 모르고 덤벼들었다가 다들 기어서 돌아갔다니까요. 그래서 알 만한 사람들은 언니가 젓가락을 머리에 꽂는다 싶으면 그냥 내빼기 바빠. 기회를 놓친 사람들은 이렇게 말하죠. 오늘, 집에, 다 갔다.

아휴, 이 사람들은 어째 이런 얘기에 더 신 나 해. 꼭 교생 첫사랑 얘기 듣는 여고생 표정이잖아. 우리 독회 안 해요? 거봐, 내가 독회 끝나고 얘기한다니까. 그날 술자리요? 당연히 제가 졌죠. 게임이 되어야 말이죠. 나 그날 언니 자취방으로 실려갔잖아. 아마 언니가 업고 갔을걸? 힘도 어찌나 좋은지 여자애들 정도는 그냥 번쩍번쩍 들어. 나중에 선배들이 혀를 차요. 어디 감히 영은 언니랑 대작을 하냐고. 언니가 그런 사람인 줄 내가 어떻게 알았겠어.

멋있다구요? 멋있죠? 그래요 멋있어요. 나도 완전 반했잖아. 언니가 묘하게 사람 끌어당긴다니까. 남의 기

26

chopstick to show you what it was really like. But this pencil will have to do for now. She bunched her hair up like this, and using her left hand, twisted the bunch into a loop, and then inserted the chopstick into the loop and threaded it through the hair in and out, and then, voila! How about that? It looks like an ornamental hairpin, doesn't it? You can use another chopstick, making it cross the first one at an angle like the letter X. The whole process was done in no time flat.

You're right. It's a habit of hers. She always puts her hair up using a chopstick before she begins any serious drinking. It doesn't have to be a chopstick. She'll also use a ballpoint pen, toothbrush, or whatever can keep her hair twisted up. Oh, she's a hard drinker all right. Once she starts drinking in the evening, she'll continue until daybreak. Sometimes you'd wonder if she would indeed turn into *soju* if she kept at it like that. I wonder if she's still drinking that much today? Probably not, considering her age. She was young back then. When we did some volunteer work at a farming village, the young men there took up her dare but only to crawl back home in the end. So, the insiders would quickly sneak away when they saw her putting a

운을 자기 쪽으로 싸악 끌어모으면서 단번에 잡아채. 알고 보면 무서운 사람이지. 그러니까 매력이랄지 마력이랄지, 암튼 빠져들게 만드는 힘이 있어요. 연애요? 학교 다닐 때? 진짜 여고생들처럼 왜 그래요? 몰라요. 알아도 그걸 제가 어떻게 말해요. 사람이 의리가 있지. 정 궁금하면 작가와의 만남 때 물어봐요. 하긴, 작가 불러 놓고 그런 거 물어보면 실례겠지? 물어본다고 답해줄 것도 아니고. 작품세계를 중심으로 물어봐야지. 그게 예의지.

잘은 모르지만, 학교에서 언니 좋아하는 사람 많았을 거야. 그땐 연애하는 것도 눈치 보던 시절이니까. 꽁꽁 숨어서들 했지. 그러니 난 잘 모르지. 어쨌든 언니랑 자취 같이하는 동안 둘만 조용히 밥 먹어본 적이 없어요. 사람들이 어찌나 많이 드나드는지. 자취방이 꼭 주막 같애. 아 그러니까 그 비빔국수 생각나네. 그거 진짜 맛있었는데. 언니가 해준 비빔국수. 언니가 요리하는 걸 좋아해요. 잘하기도 하고. 뭐 해 먹이는 거 진짜 좋아해. 한 명이고 열 명이고, 오는 족족 다 해먹이고. 한 손으로는 국수 삶으면서, 또 한 손으로는 양념장 만들고. 그 많

chopstick in her hair. Anyone who'd missed the chance to leave in time would say, "I'll never be able to make it home today."

Oh dear, you people have so much fun with stories like this, don't you? You look just like high-school girls listening to the first-love story of your student teacher. Aren't we gonna do the reading? I knew it! I said I'd tell you after the reading session.

That day? The drinking dare? I lost, of course. I was no match for her. I ended up back at her place. She probably carried me there on her back. She was so strong that she could lift a young woman without even trying. Later, other seniors of mine clicked their tongues. "How dare you drink with Yong-un!" How could I have known what kind of drinker she was?

Cool? Cool indeed! Yes, she was cool. She'd completely charmed me. She had this uncanny ability to draw people to her. She channels other people's energy in her direction and instantly captivates them. She may even frighten you, once you know her well. Such is her charm, her bewitchment. She just had this power to attract you. Love affairs? On campus? Shame on you, asking a ques-

은 면을 양재기에 휙휙 비벼서 뚝딱! 자취방 양념 가지고 어쩜 그렇게 입에 짝짝 붙게 만들어내는지. 골뱅이 통조림이라도 하나 넣어봐요, 아주 양재기에 달라붙어 가지고는 그냥. 아우 생각만 해도 군침 돈다.

그러고 보니 얼마 전에 언니 산문집도 나왔네. 음식 산문집. 근데 거기 비빔국수 얘긴 안 나오더라. 하긴 그게 스페인에 머물면서 먹었던 음식들 위주로 쓴 거니까 나올 리가 없지. 언니는 비빔국수나 청국장, 홍어무침 뭐 이런 게 더 어울리는데. 구수하게 사람 냄새 나는. 난 작가들이 와인이니 커피니 아스파라거스 곁들인 어쩌구저쩌구하는 거 좀 닭살 돋더라. 그야말로 옛날 여류 작가 필이야. 맞죠? 아무리 생각해봐도 언니는 비빔국수 이런 거 더 어울리는데. 내가 언니한테 붙여준 별명이 있거든요.

고물상주인. 네, 고물상이요. 고민고물상이라고나 할까? 고민을 가지고 언니한테 가면, 언니는 그 고민을 들여다본 다음에 뭐든 줘요. 해결책을 주거나 방향을 제시해주거나 위안을 주거나. 그러니까 이런 거죠. 찌그러진 깡통을 들고 갔더니 설탕을 주네? 깨진 병을 들고

tion like that, just like a bunch of high-school girls. I don't know. Even if I knew, how could I tell you about it myself? I'm a woman of loyalty, you know. If you really want to know, then ask her when you meet her at the Meet the Writer session. Come to think of it, it'd be rude to ask that sort of question to a guest writer, wouldn't it? Not that she'd answer the question, even if you asked. Your questions should center on her work. We shouldn't forget our manners.

I'm not quite sure. But I believe there were many people in the university who liked her. It was a time when you had to be careful about your love affairs. It was all done in hiding. So, how could I possibly know? One thing, though, while we were sharing the room, we never quietly ate alone. There were so many visitors constantly coming and going. The room was just like an inn. Ah, that reminds me of the spicy noodles. It was really delicious. That spicy noodles Yong-un used to cook for us. She loved to cook and was a great cook, too. What she truly enjoyed, though, was feeding others. It didn't matter if there was only one or ten visitors; she used to feed them all whenever they came. She would boil noodles with one hand and

갔더니 뻥튀기를 주네? 그게 참 달고 맛있네? 뭔가 바꿔 먹는 재미가 있네? 또 가고 싶네? 없던 고민도 만들고 싶네? 딱 고물상이지 뭐야. 그죠? 내 말이 맞죠?

왜 아니겠어요. 나도 그 고물상 뻔질나게 들락거렸지. 그래서 자취도 같이하게 된 거구. 제가 집이 인천이라 학교까지 버스 타고 전철 갈아타고 두 시간 넘게 걸렸어요. 너무 힘들어하니까 그럼 방을 같이 쓰재요. 또 내가 등록금 때문에 방학 때 아르바이트를 구해야겠다고 하니까 그러지 말고 자기 밑으로 들어오래요. 아, 총여학생회요. 언니가 편집부장이었거든. 영은 언니는 총여학생회 편집부장, 나는 편집부원. 그리고 학생회 간부 장학금까지. 원래 편집부원한테는 안 주는 건데, 언니가 어떻게 해가지고 되게 만들었어요.

그러니까 우리는 안 친하려야 안 친할 수가 없었지. 방도 같이 쓰죠, 학교 가면 같이 앉아서 회지 만들죠, 또 세미나도 같이하죠. 언니 동생 같다고 할까, 엄마 딸 같다고 할까. 암튼 딱 붙어 다녔다니까. 농활도 같이 가고 기지촌 여성 봉사활동도 가고. 진짜 많이 다녔다. 받기도 많이 받고. 음…… 그렇다고 받기만 한 건 아녜요.

prepare sauce with the other. Then she would mix the huge amount of noodles with the sauce in a big enamel-bowl, her hand a blur. And, what a divine-tasting sauce she used to make, using only what was available in our room. When she added to it something like a can of sea snails, we licked our bowls clean... Wow! Just thinking about it makes my mouth water.

By the way, her essay collection came out not long ago. A collection of food-related essays. But there's no essay on that spicy-noodle dish in it. In fact, the essays are mainly about the foods she ate while traveling in Spain; so, the spicy noodles can't be part of that collection. To be honest, foods like the spicy noodles, fermented soybean soup, and seasoned thornback better become Yong-un. I mean more rustic foods, smelling of the ordinary people. I get gooseflesh all over when I hear writers talking about wine and coffee and dishes garnished with asparagus blah blah blah... It's really what the women writers of the bygone times would have talked about. Don't you agree? The more I think about it, the more I'm convinced that things like spicy noodles suit her better. You know what? I even gave her a nickname.

왜요, 나도 많이 췄죠. 이를테면…… 왜 그 소설 있잖아요. 할머니랑 손녀랑 닭 잡아먹는 얘기. 노래하는 꽃마차. 맞아요. 그거 제가 해준 얘기거든요? 거기 나온 손녀가 바로 저예요. 자취방에서 둘이 닭 시켜먹다가, 내가 시골에서 할머니랑 닭 잡아먹던 얘기 해줬거든. 영은 언니는 닭 먹을 때 다른 거 다 놔두고 모가지 먼저 집어요. 먹잘 것도 없는 거 왜 좋아하냐니까 야들야들해서 좋대. 난 모가지 절대 안 먹는데. 그래서 그 얘기를 해줬지.

나 어릴 때 할머니랑 둘이 살았거든요. 우리 할머니가 촌부여도 되게 고운 양반이었어요. 섬세하고 예쁜 거 좋아하고. 그래서 닭은 키우는데 정작 잡아먹지를 못하는 거야. 알은 자꾸만 까고 닭은 점점 늘어가고, 한 스무 마리 되었을걸? 하루는 내가 닭고기가 너무 먹고 싶어서 막 졸랐어. 어쩔 수 있나. 잡아야지. 근데 할머니는 닭 뒤만 졸졸 쫓아다니면서 잡지를 못해. 그래서 내가 나섰잖아. 열 살 땐가? 그냥 닭 목을 콱 잡고 비틀었어

Secondhand dealer. Yes, like an owner of secondhand store—a store that takes the troubles and worries of other people off of their hands. When you took your trouble to her, she'd look into it and then give you something else in exchange for it. A solution or direction or consolation.

It worked like this. You'd bring her a crumpled can, and she'd give you sugar. You'd bring her a broken bottle, and she'd give you popped rice. Ah, it tasted so good. It was fun to trade with her. You wanted to visit her store again. You even felt like faking your troubles. See? She definitely was secondhand dealer. Right? I'm making sense, aren't I?

Of course, I am. I frequented the secondhand dealer many times myself. That's how we ended up sharing the room. I lived in Incheon and it took over two hours to reach school, first taking the bus and then transferring to the electric train. When she saw I was having a hard time, she suggested that we share the room. That's not all. When I told her I needed to look for a part-time job during the school holidays to save money for my tuition, she told me to work for her. Ah, she had a position in the General Girl Students Association. As the chief editor. Yes, Yong-un was the General Women Stu-

요. 그 어린애가. 그러게요, 진짜 닭고기가 좋았나 봐. 아님 뭘 모르는 어린애니까 그랬겠지? 지금 잡으라면 그걸 어떻게 잡아. 아무튼 그렇게 해서 닭을 잡아먹기는 먹었는데요, 털 벗기면서 보니까 이 닭 모가지가 다 으스러져 있어. 손에 얼마나 힘을 줬는지. 그런데 보통은 그런 일 있으면 닭고기 안 먹게 되잖아요? 그래도 난 닭고기가 너무 맛있어. 아직도 좋아해요. 단, 모가지는 안 먹어요. 이 얘기 해주니까 영은 언니가 진짜 재밌어 하는 거예요. 모가지를 쭉쭉 빨면서. 뼈 마디마디를 다 해체해보면서, 몇 번이나 물어보더라구.

아깝기는요, 내 추억이 맛있는 소설로 되살아났는데. 나더러 쓰라면 그렇게 못 쓰죠. 언니니까 쓰지. 그리고 소설가가 어떻게 자기 경험한 것만 골라서 써요. 듣고서 꼭 경험한 것처럼 쓰기도 하는 거지. 소설이 뭐 별거야? 세상에 떠도는 얘기를 수집해서 그럴싸하게 재구성하는 거지. 그것도 능력이지. 안 그래요? 그리고 고물상 주인이 물 퍼다 장사해요? 돈이 되니까 고물도 수집하는 거지. 병이든 깡통이든 다 쓸모가 없으면 그걸 왜 받겠어. 어머나 내가 미쳤나 봐. 혼자 떠들고 있었네. 이

dent Association's chief editor and I was a member of the editorial staff. On top of that, I received a scholarship as one of the executive members of the Students Association. Normally, ordinary members of the editorial staff weren't eligible for that scholarship. Yong-un somehow managed to get me one.

So, we were bound to grow close. We shared the room, made the bulletin together at school, and belonged to the same seminars. We were like sisters. Or, like mother and daughter. Anyway, we were together all the time. We did our volunteer work together, helping farmers in the countryside and women in the military camp-side towns. We did so many things together. She gave so much to me. Well... It's not that I was always taking from her. Why, I gave her a lot, too. For example...

One of her stories! You probably know it. The one about a grandmother and granddaughter slaughtering and eating a chicken. "Singing Flower Wagon." Yes, that's the one. I told her the story. The granddaughter in that story is me. One day, we had fried chicken delivered to our room. While we were eating, I told her the story of my grandmother and me slaughtering a chicken and eating it to-

러려고 한 게 아닌데. 기억이라는 게, 이게 고구마처럼, 한번 뽑아 올리면 줄줄이 따라오게 돼 있잖아요. 아이고 죄송해요. 시간 가는 줄도 모르고.

아, 언니 이력? 그게 참 특이하죠? 사 년제 대학 나와서 소설 공부하겠다고 다시 전문대 들어가고, 그래서 소설가가 되기까지, 그냥 소설이 나를 이끌었다, 정말 드라마 같지 않아요? 내가 잘 알죠, 그때, 언니가 그 결정 내릴 때. 언니가 학교에서 매정하게 등 돌리던 순간. 다들 배신자라고 언니한테 뭐라고 하고.

그러니까 그게, 그때 학교에요, 학생회 활동 이런 거 말구, 좀 비밀스러운 조직이 있었어요. 운동권이요? 에이 뭐, 운동권이라기보다는, 그냥 철학 공부 좀 하고 세미나도 하고 학교 걱정도 나누고. 아무튼 난 사실 왕년에 운동권이었네 하는 사람들 말 하나도 안 믿어요. 돌 몇 번 던진 거 가지고서는 운동권입네. 그러면 뭔가 좀 의식 있어 보이나? 뭐가 자랑스럽다고. 사실 옛날 운동권들 하는 게 꼭 피라미드 장사 같지 않아요? 사람 장

gether. Yong-un always ate the chicken neck first before all the other parts. I asked her why she liked the neck with its scant bits of meat. She said she liked it because the meat on it was soft and moist. I never eat chicken necks. So, I told her the story.

When I was a little girl, I lived with my grandmother. The countrywoman she was, my grandmother was a gentle person. She was fond of delicate, pretty things. She bred chickens for food, but she couldn't bring herself to slaughter them. The chicks kept hatching and the number of chickens grew greater and greater.

The incident happened when there were about twenty of them. One day, I wanted to eat chicken meat so bad, so I started nagging her. My grandmother had no choice but to try to slaughter one. So she try chasing a chicken down but she could never catch it. So, I volunteered to do it myself. I was probably around ten. I just grabbed the chicken's neck and gave it a quick twist. Yes, I was a mere child. I know what you mean. I must have liked chicken that much. Or, maybe I was just too young to know any better, perhaps? If I was asked

사. 황홀한 미래가 있는 것처럼 꼬드겨서 사람들 모으고, 그 사람들이 또 사람들 모으고. 사람이 힘이다,라는 게 결국 사람이 돈이다,라는 거지. 또 진짜로 그 운동권 떨거지들이 피라미드 많이 했어요. 운동한답시고 성적도 안 좋고 취직도 안 되니까 방법이 있나. 시스템 비슷하기도 하고. 아무튼 그게 중요한 건 아니구.

어느 날, 언니가 나더러 자정까지 어디로 오래. 어디로 가니까 누가 나와서 또 어디로 데려가요. 그래서 어디에 도착했는데 사람들이 주르르 앉아 있어. 아는 사람도 있고 모르는 사람도 있고, 같이 세미나 하던 동기 얼굴도 보이고. 뭐랄까 엄숙하면서 약간 으스대는 분위기? 진짜 놀란 거는요, 졸업도 못 하고 애들한테 빌붙어서 밥이나 얻어먹던 껄렁껄렁한 선배 하나가 있었는데, 바로 그 사람이 조직의 좌장이라는 거야. 거기다가 외부에 더 큰 조직과 연결되어 있다 하고. 그게 북이라고 믿는 애들도 있고. 지금 생각하면 순진했던 거지. 멍청했던 건가? 그땐 나도 뭐 그런가 부다 했지. 어쨌든 그날 나까지 포함해서 여섯 명이 그 조직에 합류하게 된 거예요. 환영식이라고 해야 할지 서약식이라고 해야 할

to do it again now, I don't think I could do it.

As I plucked the dead chicken, I found that its neck bones had all been crushed. I must have squeezed it awfully hard. After experiencing something like that, most people would avoid eating chicken. Right? But I still love chicken. It's so delicious. I don't eat the necks, though. Yong-un truly relished this story at the time. She slurped at the neck and noisily took all the bones apart and then asked me to repeat the details of the story several times.

Regret? Not at all. Not when my memory has been reborn as a delicious novel. I wouldn't be able to write a better story myself, even though it's from my own memory. It takes someone like Yong-un to do that. Moreover, writers need more than their personal experiences to produce their works. They may write about what they've heard from others, making it sound like their own first-hand experience. What's fiction anyway? They're the stories that go around in the world, collected and reconstructed in such a way that the outcomes sound plausible. That takes talent, too. Don't you agree? You don't think the owners of secondhand stores invest nothing in their businesses, do you?

지, 암튼 그런 것도 하고. 거기 한가운데서 언니는 흐뭇하게 웃고 있고. 그때 뭐랄까, 내가 완전히 언니 사람이 되었다는 느낌? 그러면서도 내가 언니에 대해 모르는 게 많았구나 싶으면서 섭섭한 느낌? 아무튼 좀 복잡했어요.

환영식 끝나고 다음 해 학생회 선거 얘기를 하기 시작하는데, 문제는 거기서 발생한 거예요. 조직에서는 언니가 당연히 5학년으로 남아서 총여학생회장으로 출마할 거라고 생각하고 있었대요. 그 전해부터 계획된 일이었대요. 피디 진영조차 언니를 상대로 염두에 두고 후보를 물색하고 있었다니까. 그땐 5학년 6학년 남아서 학생운동 하는 거 흔했거든. 아니면 학교 나가 현장으로 투입되든가. 그런데 언니가 졸업을 한다는 거야. 졸업도 졸업인데 글쎄 현장도 아니고 전혀 다른 일을 하겠다는 거야. 그래요. 소설. 소설을 쓰겠다고. 다른 방식의 운동이라나 뭐라나. 학교는 후배들이 잘 알아서 할 거라고. 누군가 물었죠. 그런데 졸업이 돼? 언니는 고개만 끄덕끄덕. 그동안 언니가 계절학기를 들어가며 학점을 채우고 있었던 걸 아무도 몰랐던 거야. 난리가 났잖

They buy junk because it'll make them some profit. Why would they collect empty bottles and cans if they were completely useless? Goodness, I must be out of my mind. I've been rambling on and on. I didn't mean to. Memories are like sweet potatoes. You can never dig one out without having others on the rootstock tag along one after another. I'm so sorry. I've lost track of time.

Ah, her career? It's very peculiar, isn't it? After graduating from the university, she entered a college to study creative writing. From then on, she was led by Muse herself until she became a writer. Dramatic story, isn't it? I know the situation well. I was there when she made that decision. When she turned her back on all of us at school. Everyone criticized her. Called her a traitor.

I'm talking about the situation that the universities were in back then. Among the many campus activities, there were some secret organizations that were distinctly set apart from the students associations. Student activists? Well, not really activists; they were actually just some students who studied philosophy and held seminars together and shared their concerns about the campus situation. In any

아요. 기회주의자에 배신자라고. 언니가 등을 돌린 건 사실이니까. 아무 대책도 마련해놓지 않고. 뒤도 안 돌아보고 가겠다는 거잖아. 책임도 안 지고. 조직 입장에서 당연히 배신이지. 나한테도 배신이고. 타이밍 한번 절묘했잖아? 나를 조직 안으로 들여놓은 때, 언니는 밖으로 나가겠다고 선언을 하고. 그걸 그냥 공교롭다고만 볼 수도 없고.

아, 물론 저도 그걸 배신이라고 생각지는 않아요. 다른 사람이 그렇게 생각했다는 거지. 그럼요, 그게 어떻게 배신이야. 나는 무조건 지지했지요. 사람이 한번 믿으면 끝까지 믿어줘야지. 내가 나서서 조직 사람들 다 설득하고 그랬으니까 됐지. 나 아니었으면 언니 완전 매장당했을 거야. 사실 언니 선택이 뭐가 문제겠어요. 그 시절이 이상했던 거지. 희생이 절대가치구 정의가 나침반이구 대의에서 벗어난 작은 목소리는 개인주의구 어쩌구저쩌구. 그러니까 언니 선택은 배신이라기보다는 그 이상한 시절로부터의 탈출이지. 맞아요, 탈출.

case, I don't trust a word of what any self-professed former student activist says. Calling yourself an activist for tossing a few rocks in the past. As if that would make you look more class-conscious. What's there to be proud of? In fact, when you think about it, don't you think what the student activists did back then is quite similar to what pyramid marketing systems do now? Human trade. Collecting and amassing human assets by seducing them with fantastic visions. Then, the seduced in turn seduce others, and so on.

"People are power" means "People are money," after all. To tell the truth, a lot of those so-called student activists actually joined pyramid organizations. They failed to get good grades thanks to their activist work; consequently, couldn't get any jobs. So, that was their last resort. They may have found the two systems similar... Never mind, that's not important now.

One day, Yong-un asked me to meet her around midnight. When I found my way to our arranged meeting place, a stranger came and took me somewhere else. When I finally arrived, I saw many people sitting in line. I knew some of them. One was my contemporary who had done a seminar

그게 어떻게 배신이야. 탈출을 했으니까 소설가도 된 거지. 그럼요, 당연히 배신이, 아니,죠. 그런데 언니가 무슨 빚을 졌냐구요? 그 배신을 말하는 거냐구요? 아니에요. 그런 게 뭐가 빚이에요. 학교 다닐 때 일 가지고. 그런 거 말구…… 있어요. 아무튼. 그런 게. 옛날얘기는 이제 그만하죠.

와주겠죠. 언니가 그렇게 매정한 사람도 아니고, 제가 부탁하는데, 들어주겠죠. 아무리 바빠도. 와줄 거예요. 그런데 너무 기대는 마세요. 아니요. 안 된다는 게 아니라, 기대가 크면 실망도 그만큼 크니까, 기대는 하지 말고. 아무튼 내일 영은 언니 만나면 잘 부탁해볼게요. 그런데 만약에 언니가, 아니 서진 작가가 온다고 하면, 강연료는 줘야겠죠? 그야말로 거마비라도? 아님 선물 같은 거 준비할까요? 무슨 선물이 좋을까요?

*

우리 몇 년 만이에요? 언니 하나도 안 변했네. 지면으로 자주 봐서 그런가? 어제 헤어지고 다시 만나는 거 같

with me. How should I describe the atmosphere? Solemn. And yet—a bit overbearing, maybe?

The real shock was yet to come. There was a totally untrustworthy senior student who had failed to graduate and who completely leeched off other students. I was told this student was the foreman of that group. Furthermore, he was said to be connected to a larger organization outside. Some believed it was North Korea. Now, I can see how naive we all were. Or, were we simply stupid? Back then, I was no exception; I believed anything I was told.

Anyhow, that day, six in total, including myself, joined the organization. There was even a procedure to either welcome or swear us new members in. Yong-un was in the center of it all. She was smiling. At that time, I felt... How should I put it? I felt that I wholly belonged among her people. At the same time, I felt disappointed, realizing that there was so much I didn't know about her. My feelings were complicated.

After the welcoming ceremony, we began talking about the next year's election for the Students Association when a problem arose. The organization never doubted that Yong-un would stay on as a

아. 그런데 언니가 먼저 연락을 다 해주시고. 좀 놀랐어요. 반갑지 않다는 게 아니라, 맨날 내가 먼저 전화했는데 언니가 이렇게 먼저 전화해서 만나자고 해주니까. 놀라기도 하고 무슨 일 있나 걱정도 되고. 원래 나이 들어서 오랜만에 걸려온 전화 나가보면, 정수기 사라느니 보험 들라느니, 그런 거잖아. 청첩장 보낸다는 나이는 지나도 벌써 지났구. 물론 언니 전화가 그렇다는 게 아니라. 나야 너무너무 고맙지. 언니 책 따라 읽고 기사로도 보니까 대략 잘 지내고 계시는구나 하면서도, 정작 연락은 못 하겠더라구요. 애 키우느라 정신도 없었구요. 참 우리 애, 학교 들어갔어요. 나 학부형이야. 안 믿어지죠? 세월 참 빨라요. 그쵸?

그런데 왜 만나자고 하셨어요? 무슨 특별한 일이 있으신 거예요? 요즘에요? 글쎄 뭐 요즘이라고 별다를 건 없지만, 뭐 좀 변화가 있었다면, 저 대학원 들어갔어요. 우리 신랑이 하고 싶은 거 다 하고 살라구 밀어줘서. 뒤늦게 학위 받으러 간 건 아니구요. 그냥 뭐, 학교 다닐 때 공부 안 하고 딴짓만 해서. 공부 좀 해볼까 하구. 왜 언니도 학교 졸업하고 전문대 다시 들어갔잖아요.

48

fifth-year student and run for the chairperson of the General Women Students Association. It had already been penciled in the previous year. Even the PD camp was already looking for a candidate who could be a match for Yong-un. At the time, it was common for students to stay on in university for an extra year or two to continue their activities in their student movements. Or, they would graduate and would join the field. But then, Yong-un surprised all of us by declaring that she was planning to graduate. That's not all. She said she wouldn't work in the field, either. She wanted to do something completely different. Yes, she wanted to be a fiction writer. She claimed it was a different style of activism. School would be well taken care of by her juniors, according to her.

Someone asked her: "By the way, are you even eligible for graduation?" She nodded in silence.

No one knew she'd taken courses during the summer and winter sessions to fulfill the credit requirements for graduation. There was hullabaloo.

She was called an opportunist and traitor. There was no denying that she'd turned her back on the rest of us. She hadn't prepared any countermeasures. And yet, she insisted on leaving without

아 참, 말이 나와서 말인데요? 저 언니한테 부탁이 있
어요. 꼭 들어주셔야 돼요. 들어주신다고 해주세요, 네?
실은요, 제가 몇몇 사람들하고 독서토론회를 하거든요.
별건 아니지만, 제가 거기 회장이에요. 국어교사도 있
고, 미술 하는 사람도 있고, 다양해요. 그런데 이번에 언
니 작품 가지고 토론회 했거든요. 우리 회원들이 언니
소설 진짜 좋아해. 완전 광팬들이야. 언니 얼굴 한번 꼭
보고 싶대. 그래서 언니가 초청강연을 해줬으면 하는
데. 그냥 한 시간 정도, 언니 작품 얘기 해주시고, 뭐 작
가로 살아가는 얘기. 부담 가지실 필요는 없구요. 많지
는 않지만 강연료도 있어요. 나, 언니랑 친하다고 막 자
랑했단 말야. 친하다고 하니까 사람들이 안 믿잖아. 언
니가 안 오면 거짓말했다고 생각할 거 아냐. 회장 체면
말이 아니지. 맨날 자랑하는 것두 아니구. 마침 언니한
테 전화도 오고 그래서 처음 자랑한 거예요. 진짜예요.
여태 한 마디도 안 했어. 언니한테 누 될까 봐. 그러니까
언니, 부탁해요, 네? 시간은 언니한테 맞출게. 꼭 이번
달이 아니어도 돼요. 올해 안에만. 그래 올해 안에. 딱
한 시간만. 네? 언니, 우리 친한 거 맞잖아. 아니에요?

looking back. Refused to take any responsibility. From the organization's point of view, her decision was most definitely an act of betrayal. She'd betrayed me, too. And perfect timing, perhaps? As soon as she placed me inside the organization, she declared her departure from it. It was hard to consider it a mere coincidence.

Ah, of course, I don't think she betrayed me. It's just that other people thought that she did. Yes, of course. How could that be an act of betrayal? I supported her decision unconditionally. Once I trust someone, I trust that person for good. I volunteered to persuade all the other people in the organization for her. Without me, she would have become a complete outcast. As a matter of fact, nothing was wrong with her choice. Something was wrong with the time itself. Sacrifice was the absolute highest value. Justice was our compass. The smaller voices outside the grand cause belonged to individualism. Blah blah blah.

Her choice wasn't a betrayal but an escape from that strange time. Yes, an escape. That couldn't have been a betrayal. Because she escaped, she became a writer. Needless to say: IT. WAS. NOT. A.

나만 그렇게 생각하고 있었던 건가? 제발요, 네? 네? 네, 그래요. 일단 한번 생각해보세요.

이 집 스파게티 정말 맛있다. 언니가 미각이 뛰어나니까 맛집도 잘 아는구나. 다음엔 제가 모실게요. 우리 신랑이랑 언제 밥 한번 같이 먹어요. 우리 신랑두 언니 왕팬이잖아. 맨날 나한테 물어봐. 언니작가 잘 있냐고. 우리 신랑이 잘 가는 스시 집이 있는데, 거기 진짜 최고거든? 유명한 작가랑 가면 더 잘해주겠지. 꼭 한번 같이 가요. 그런데 언니 다음 책은 언제 나와요? 장편소설이에요? 그러니까 세 번째 장편인 거죠? 너무 기대된다. 무슨 얘기예요? 언니는 연애소설 같은 거 안 써요? 연애소설 쓰면 진짜 대박 날 거야.

언니 첫 책 나왔을 때 생각나요. 나 괜히 서점 기웃기웃하면서 사람들이 좀 사가나 살펴보고, 언니 책 잘 보이는 데다 얹어놓고 막 그랬는데. 선물할 곳 있으면 다 언니 책으로 했잖아. 열 권도 넘게 샀을걸? 열 권이 뭐야. 학교 사람들한테 일일이 전화해서 언니 책 나왔다

BETRAYAL.

So why then, do I say that she owes me? You're asking if I wasn't referring to that betrayal all along? Oh, no. How could that kind of thing be a debt now? It's just something that happened long ago when we were in school. I'm just saying there's something else... At any rate, let's stop talking about the past.

She'll come. She's not so cold-hearted. And it's a request from none other than me. So, she'll accept the invitation. No matter how busy she is, she'll come. But please, don't get your hopes up. No, I don't mean that it won't happen. The higher your hopes are, the greater your disappointment will be. So, don't expect too much. Anyway, when I see Yong-un tomorrow, I'll try my best to make her say yes. But if Yong-un—no—if So Jin agrees to come, we should give her an honorarium, shouldn't we? At least, for the horses and vehicles, as it were? Or, should we get her a gift of some sort? What should we get her then?

*

How long has it been? You haven't changed a bit.

고 알려주고. 내가 책을 냈어도 그렇게 못 하지. 인터뷰 기사 오려서 스크랩도 해놨는데. 그거 찾아보면 어디 있을 테니까 혹시 필요하면 말씀하세요. 선물로 드릴게요. 원래 자기 기사 스크랩하고 이런 거 본인은 못 할 거 아냐. 민망해서.

그때는 언니한테 연락하고 싶은 걸 꾹 참았잖아요. 책에 사인도 받고 그러고 싶었는데. 언니한테 연락했을 때가, 아마 언니 두 번째 책 나온 직후였을 거야. 전화하면서 은근 걱정했잖아요. 언니가 나 기억 못 하면 어떻게 처신해야 하나. 왜 그런 사람들 있잖아. 좀 유명해졌다 싶으면 옛날 지인들 무시하고. 좀 걱정은 됐지만 설마 영은 언니가 그러겠어? 하면서 전화를 걸었죠. 그리고 물었죠. 언니, 저 기억하세요? 미경이에요. 그랬더니 언니는 곧바로 김미경? 하고 되물었어. 막 반가워하면서. 언니가 아는 사람만 해도 열 명이 넘는다던 그 흔한 미경이들 중에서, 내가 어떤 설명도 하지 않았는데, 단박에, 이 김미경이를, 알아내주다니. 내 목소리에 김미경이를 연상시키는 특별한 게 있나? 아니면 언니가 목소리랑 사람을 연결시키는 특별한 재주가 있나? 어쨌

Is it because I've seen your pictures in papers and books so often? It feels like we've never separated. By the way, I was so surprised to hear from you. Not that I'm not happy to see you again. I've always been the one to call you, but this time, you called me first and wanted to see me. I was half surprised and half worried that there might be something wrong with you. You know those phone calls we, at our age, get from a friend we haven't heard from in ages? You go out to see the friend only to hear her sales pitch for a water purifier or an insurance policy. You know what I mean. We're too old to send our wedding invitations. I'm not saying that your call was one of them. I'm very, very grateful that you called. I've been reading your books and the articles about you, so I've always known that you were well. But, I haven't been able to call you. I've been so busy myself raising my child. By the way, my kid's started elementary school. I'm now a parent of a student. It's hard to believe, isn't it? Time flies, right?

Anyway, what did you want to see me for? Is there something you wanted to tell me? Me? Lately? Well, there hasn't been much change in my life. Except that I've joined a graduate program. My

거나 언니는 내 기대를 배반하지 않았지요. 그래서 만났죠, 우리. 시내에서 밥 먹고 거기 덕수궁 안에 있는 미술관도 가고. 무슨 남미 작가 작품 전시하고 있었는데. 정말 옛날로 다시 돌아간 거 같았어. 그때 나 소설 쓰고 싶다고 언니한테 처음 말했지. 문화센터에서 소설공부 하고 있다고. 그랬더니 언니가 수첩도 줬잖아요. 몇 장 안 쓴 거라고, 가방에서 바로 꺼내서 줬어. 그 뭐야, 몰스킨인가, 헤밍웨이가 썼다는 그거. 요즘에야 개나 소나 다 쓰지만, 그땐 참 대단해 보였는데. 그거 나 지금도 간직하고 있어요. 정말이에요.

네? 블로그요? 글쎄요, 요즘 그런 거 많이 하대요? 카메라들 하나씩 갖고 다니면서 자기 먹은 거 찍고 놀러 간 거 찍고 아줌마들 집 꾸미는 거 냉장고 정리하는 거 별거별거 다 올리잖아. 전 뭐 집안 살림에 워낙 소질이 없어서. 아시잖아요. 음식 맛도 잘 모르고 만드는 건 더 못하고. 그런데 왜들 그렇게 보여주고 싶어서 안달인지 몰라. 그냥 혼자 즐기면 되는 거지. 아 참, 언니 얼마 전에 파리 다녀오셨다면서요? 기사 봤어요. 프랑스어로 출판되었다구. 정말 축하해요. 이제 세계적인 작가가

husband encourages me to do whatever I want to. To get my degree before it's too late. It's just, I was never a serious student at school, always distracted by this and that. So, I want to give it another try. You also entered college after graduating from our university, didn't you?

Ah, our talk about school reminds me of a favor I need to ask of you. You have to say yes. Tell me you'll say yes, please? It's like this: I and several other people have been reading and discussing books together. It's a small-scale book club. I'm its chairperson. There's a Korean language teacher and a painter and so on, from various walks of life. This time, we're reading your works. Our members really love your novels. They're huge fans of your stories. They're dying to meet you in person. So, I'm wondering if you can be our guest lecturer. About an hour, that's all. You can talk about your works, your life as a writer, things like that. It won't be burdensome. It's not much, but you'll receive an honorarium.

I've told them you and I are very close. But they didn't believe me. If you don't come, they'll think that I've lied to them, won't they? As a chairperson, I'll lose face. I'd never bragged about it until you

되시려나 봐요. 너무 멋지고도 아름다운 일이에요. 그
렇게 유명해지면 사람들이 막 알아보고 그러지 않아
요? 사인도 해달라구 하구. 아무 데나 못 다닐 거 같아.
연예인들처럼. 맘 놓고 연애도 못 하구. 그런데 언니 결
혼은 안 해요? 사귀는 사람 없어요? 왜 없겠어. 남자들
이 줄을 섰겠지. 그런데 언니 아직 거기 살아요? 녹번동
인가? 그쪽 언저리 지나갈 때마다 언니 생각했는데. 혹
시 언니가 장이라도 봐서 지나가지는 않을까 하면서.

　그런 블로그 말고 뭐요? 아, 책 읽어주는 여자? 알아
요. 그쪽에선 꽤 유명할걸요? 가차 없잖아. 재밌기도 하
고. 기발하기도 하고. 누군지 모르지만 참 센스 있어. 얼
굴 없는 블로거라고 다들 궁금해하고. 뭐 몇 명이 분야
별로 나눠서 쓴다는 소문도 있고. 왜요? 언니 블로그 시
작하게요? 언니 그런 거 안 하잖아요. 하긴 독자들이 좋
아하긴 할 거야. 뭔가 속살 들여다보는 것 같구. 혹시 그
것 땜에 저 만나자고 하신 거예요? 내가 도움이 되려
나? 내가 뭘 알아야지. 에이, 언니는 그냥 지금처럼 해
요. 뒤늦게 뭐 그런 거 뛰어들려구. 그래도 하고 싶으시
면, 글쎄, 누구 소개시켜줄 만한 사람이 없을까? 음……

called me the other day. Then I told them all about us for the first time. I'd never talked about you before that day. Because I didn't want to bring any trouble to you. So, please. I'm begging you. Okay? I'll let you decide the date and time. It doesn't have to be this month. As long as it's this year. Yes, before the end of this year. Just one hour, please! We're close, aren't we? Am I wrong? Is it only me who thinks that? I'm begging you. Please. Please. Please. Okay. You'll think about it, promise?

The spaghetti here is really delicious. You've got such a delicate palate, so you know the good restaurants. Next time, it's my treat. Let me and my husband take you to a nice restaurant. My husband's a devoted fan of yours, too. He always asks me how my writer sister's doing. There's a sushi restaurant, which is my husband's favorite. It's the best of the best. If I show up with a famous writer, the service will be even better. We have to go there sometime together. When's your next book coming out? Is it a full-length novel? Then, it'll be your third full-length novel, right? I'm looking forward to it. What's it about? Do you ever write any love stories? If you do, I'm sure they'll be a huge hit.

글쎄요. 그 블로그 주인이 누군지 그걸 제가 어떻게 알겠어요.

　나요? 내가 그 블로그 운영자라고요? 그럴리가요. 누가 그래요? 인터넷 서점에서요? 내가? 그쪽에서 정말 그렇게 말했어요? 아이 참. 비밀을 지켜달라고 했더니, 그걸 말하네. 신비주의로 가려고 했는데, 소문이 좀 났나? 그래요. 저 맞아요. 제가 그 블로그 주인이에요. 뭘 그런 걸 언니한테 일일이 얘기를 해요. 그간 연락도 없었잖아. 또 그깟 블로그 가지고 뭐 자랑할 게 있다구.
　그런데요, 이게 제 자랑이 아니라요, 제 블로그가 인기가 좀 많아요. 그쪽 바닥에서는 이름도 좀 있고. 나도 그렇게까지 인기가 있을지 몰랐지. 그냥 열심히 읽고 감상평 써서 올리다 보니까 사람들이 자꾸 들어와 보대? 그러다 보니 언제부턴가 블로그 앞에 파워가 붙대? 파워가 붙으니까 대접이 달라지대? 출판사들도 이제 신간 나오면 거의 다 보내줘요. 신문에 광고하는 것보다 내 리뷰 파급 효과가 더 좋다면서. 문학 담당 기자들

I remember when your first book came out. I hung around in bookstores to see if your book sold well, and moved it to a conspicuous spot on the display shelf. I bought so many copies and gave them out as gifts. More than ten copies, I think. What am I talking about? I bought a lot more than that, come to think of it. I called every one I knew at school and told them your book had just come out. I couldn't have done any better if it had been my own book. I clipped your interview articles and kept them in a scrapbook. I still have them at home, so if you ever need it, just tell me. I'll find them and give them to you as a present. I guess it might be embarrassing for a writer to keep the clippings of the articles about herself.

I was dying to call you the other day. It was so hard to resist the temptation. I wanted to have you autograph my copy of the book. It was probably right after your second book came out that I contacted you. I was worried when I made that phone call. Wondering what I would do if you didn't remember me. You know those kinds of people. Once they're famous, they ignore their old friends. I worried a bit, but I made that call any way thinking, "Yong-un, my sister, she couldn't possibly be

도 내 리뷰 인용하고 그래. 어떨 땐 그냥 막 갖다 쓰더라구. 출처도 안 밝히고. 기회 잡아서 뭐라 해야 할까 봐. 소송을 걸든가. 아무튼 인터넷 서점에는 내 리뷰 올리는 고정 코너도 있어요. 원고료도 줘요. 돈이 중요한 건 아니구. 그깟 원고료 얼마나 된다구. 푼돈이지. 행사 때마다 초대도 하고 그러는데, 난 얼굴 잘 안 내밀어요. 그냥 글로만 보여주지. 글 쓰는 사람이 글로만 존재해야지, 자꾸 행사에 의존하면 안 되잖아.

아무튼 이게 다 언니 덕분이에요. 소설은 못 쓰지만, 그래도 책 읽고 뭔가 끄적이는 습관이 생겨서. 언니가 준 그 수첩에다 열심히 적고. 언니가 무조건 글로 남기라고 충고해줬잖아. 그래서 블로그 만들어가지고 올리기 시작한 거야. 진짜진짜, 언니 덕분이에요. 언니 세 번째 책 나온 거 리뷰 올린 게 컸죠. 그걸로 무슨 리뷰 대회 우수상도 받았어요. 그러고 보니까 그때부터 유명해지기 시작했나 보다. 내가 다시 읽어봐도 그 리뷰 정말 좋아. 언니 소설은 내가 다 따라 읽었으니까, 어디 소설뿐이겠어요? 인터뷰 기사랑 평론이랑 어디 강연 나가서 한 말까지 다 알고 있죠. 또 개인적으로도 취향이랑

one of those people."

I asked you, "Sister, do you remember me? I'm Mi-gyong." Then, you asked back right away, "Kim Mi-gyong?" You sounded so glad to hear my voice. Mi-gyong is such a common name. You'd told me once that you knew more than ten people with that name. Among all the Mi-gyongs you know, you recognized me, Kim Mi-gyong, right away. I didn't have to explain anything. I wondered if there's something in my voice that reminds people of me, Kim Mi-gyong. Or, you've got some talent recognizing people simply by listening to their voices?

Anyway, you didn't betray my expectations. So, we met. After having a meal together downtown, we went to a gallery in the Toksu Palace. There was an exhibition, of the works by some South American artist. It was just like the old days. I told you for the first time that I wanted to write stories. And that I was studying to be a writer at a cultural education center. Then you gave me a pocket-book, remember? You said you'd only used a few pages. You took it right out of your purse and gave it to me. It was one of those, what're they called? Moleskines? The kind Hemingway used. Now, everybody uses them. But, back then, it was such a

성격이랑 이력이랑 다 잘 알고. 언니 말대로 잘 아니까 잘 써지더라구. 대상을 장악하고 쓰면 좋은 글이 나온다고 언니가 그랬잖아요. 언니를 잘 알고 쓴 리뷰라 그런지, 글에 진정성이 있더라구. 진정성이 있으니까 읽는 사람들이 또 좋아하구. 그때 알았어요. 진정성이 이렇게 중요한 거로구나. 언니가 맨날 진정성 진정성 그랬잖아. 그게 도대체 뭔가 했는데, 언니 소설 리뷰 쓰면서 알게 되었다니까요.

소설 쓰는 거보다 재밌어요. 하고 싶은 일을 하면서 산다는 것이 이렇게 신명나는 일인지 처음 알았어요. 진짜진짜 좋아하는 일을 찾았으니까. 앞으로도 한 십 년 주먹 꽉 쥐고 달려 보려구.

왜요, 그만 드시게요? 많이 못 드시네요? 언니 그렇게 안 먹어서 살 빻나보구나. 옛날보다 한 십 킬로? 아니 더 되려나? 아무튼 지금 보기 딱 좋아요. 애를 안 나서 그런가, 몸도 꼭 처녀 같아요. 아, 같은 게 아니라 처녀지? 시집을 안 갔으니 당연히 처녀지. 그럼 저 이제 담

precious item to have. I still have it. I really do.

What's that? A blog? Well, many people do it these days. They go around carrying cameras with them and taking pictures of the foods they eat, the places they visit, the interior decorations and refrigerator organizations of housewives and so on, and then post them all up on their blogs. As for me, I'm not very good at housekeeping. You know me. No good at tasting food and worse at cooking. But then, I don't understand why they all want to display their private lives in public. Why don't they just enjoy their lives by themselves? Ah, by the way, you've been to Paris lately, haven't you? I read your article. Your book—translated and published in French. Congratulations! Now, you're gonna be a global writer. That's just splendid! Wonderful! Don't people recognize you wherever you go? And ask for your autograph? It must be hard for you to go anywhere. Just like a movie star. It can't be easy to have a love affair. Are you ever going to get married? No boyfriend? Come on. Men must be lining up to marry you. By the way, do you still live at the same place? Nokbon-dong? Whenever I pass through that area, I think of you. Hoping to see you on your way back home from grocery shopping or

배 피울게요. 언니는요? 끊었어요? 어머 끊었구나. 난 진짜 못 끊겠던데. 애 가졌을 때 딱 일 년. 그땐 저절로 끊어지더라구. 영은 언니, 그거 알아요? 나 담배, 언니 한테 배운 거. 맞아요, 언니가 가르쳐줬어, 맞다니까? 내가 뻐끔뻐끔 흉내만 내고 앉았으니까, 그렇게 피우려면 피우지 말라고, 담배 아깝다고, 그러면서 가르쳐줬잖아요. 나는 그때 언니가 지었던 표정도 기억나는데. 이거 들으면 언니도 기억날걸?

자, 여기 못돼먹은 애가 하나 있어. 떼쟁이 말썽쟁이 빌어먹을 놈이지. 이놈이 바닥에 주저앉아서 과자 내놓으라고 우네? 이 빌어먹을 놈 혼 좀 내줘야겠어. 쓰읍~ 너 안 일어나면 한 대 맞는다! 그때처럼 하는 거야. 쓰읍, 하고 숨을 들이마시고 후우. 쓰읍, 후우. 기억나죠? 정말 누구 한 대 때리고 난 것처럼 핑 돌더라구. 어쩜 그렇게 쉽게 가르쳐주는지. 알아듣기 쉽게 말하는 것도 능력이야 그쵸? 지금도 난, 담배 피울 때마다, 빌어먹을 놈들 등짝을 한 대씩 후려쳐요.

쓰읍. 언니 졸업하고 총여학생회실에서 혼자 담배 많이 피웠는데. 후우. 나 졸업할 때쯤엔 학교가 진짜 어려

something.

Not that kind of blog? What then? Oh, you mean "The Woman Who Reads for You"? Yes, I know that blog. It's quite well known in that field. It's relentless. And interesting. And, quite original, too. Whoever it is, the blogger's very perceptive. People are curious about this so-called "faceless blogger." Rumor has it that several bloggers are responsible for the contents, each managing his or her expert areas. Why do you ask? Are you planning to start a blog yourself? You're not the type to do that sort of thing. Well, readers may like it. They may feel like they're peeping into a celebrity's private life. Is that why you wanted to see me, by any chance? I'm not sure if I can help you with that. What on earth do I know about blogging? You really don't need it. You just keep doing what you're doing now. Why do you want to get in on all of that so late now? If you really want to do it, well, I wonder if there's anybody I can introduce you to. Hum... Well—how would I know who's the manager of that blog?

Me? Are you saying that I'm the manager of the blog? You're kidding! Who told you that? Internet Bookstore? Me? Did they really tell you so? Dear

왔거든. 학생회 간부라면 무슨 병자 취급이었지. 요즘에 흡연자들 대하는 거랑 똑같아. 건강에도 나쁜 걸 왜 그리 피우나? 남한테까지 피해주지 말고 저기 짱박혀서 혼자 피우지?

쓰읍. 언니랑 학교 다닐 때는 시절 좋았는데. 다들 미안해하면서 배려하고. 뭔가 대신 나서주는 사람에 대한 고마움 같은 것도 있고. 그런데 이 식당 담배도 피울 수 있고 괜찮네. 후우. 언니는 그 좋은 시절 보내고, 나 막차 태우고 도망가고. 나 배신하구 가서 언니는 소설가 되구 나는 인생 꼬이구. 뭐 특별히 꼬인 건 없지만.

언니가 배신이 아니라면 아닌 거죠. 물론 저도 언니가 배신했다고 생각 안 해요. 다른 사람들이 그런 시선으로 봤다는 거지. 언니 졸졸 따라다니더니 배신당해서 안쓰럽다고. 나더러 언니 추종자래. 추종자가 배신을 당했으니 그야말로 끈 떨어진 연이지. 아니지, 연도 없는 끈을 붙들고 있는 거지. 그게 멍충이지 뭐야. 언제 적 일인데요. 저, 다 잊었어요.

쓰읍. 근데 언니 요즘에도 젓가락 꽂고 술 마셔요? 하긴 다 젊었을 때 얘기다 그쵸? 후우. 언니 생각날 때 나

68

me! I asked them to keep it a secret, but they let on. I planned to stay mysterious, but I guess the cat's out of the bag now. Yes, it's me. I'm the owner of that blog. Well, what on earth is there to talk to you about it? We haven't even kept in touch with each other for a long while, remember? Moreover, it isn't anything to brag about.

Having said that, I don't mean to sing my own praises, but my blog is rather popular. It's made a name in that field. I didn't know it would get that popular. I just kept reading and posting my reviews. After a while, I realized people were visiting my blog fairly often. Then, one day, people started to call my blog a "power blog." Once the word "power" was attached to it, a whole different world unfolded. Now, publishers send me almost all of their new releases. They say my reviews have a better ripple effect than the newspaper ads. Even the reporters in charge of literature section cite my reviews, you see. Sometimes, they just use my writing without revealing the source. I may have to make a complaint about that when I get a chance to. Or, sue them.

Mind you, there's a corner in the Internet bookstores designated for my reviews. And I also get

도 언니처럼 젓가락으로 머리 틀어 올리고 술 마셔봤다? 그러면 술맛이 참 좋아. 왜 좋은 걸까? 젓가락 하나 꽂았을 뿐인데? 가끔 깃발 얘기도 애들한테 해주고 그랬는데, 그걸 제대로 이해하는 후배들이 없어. 다들 뭔소리냐 하는 얼굴로 쳐다봐. 하긴 요즘 애들이 인생의 유예라는 말을 어떻게 이해하겠어요. 내가 언니처럼 하니까 애들이 뭐라는 줄 알아요? 허세작렬이래요. 내가 소주가 되고 싶은지 소주가 내가 되고 싶은지, 그게 뭔말이냐고요. 요새 말로 허세가 쩐대요. 그러니까 언니때는 시절이 좋았던 거지. 젓가락을 이해하는 나 같은 후배도 있구.

이건 뭐예요? 제 블로그에 실린 글이요? 읽어봤냐구요? 어디 보자. 아…… 네, 읽어본 것 같네요. 맞아요, 읽어봤어요. 회지에 실린 내 글하고 언니 글하고 비교해놓은 글. 그 글 처음 실렸을 때 나도 깜짝 놀랐잖아요. 아, 이런 게 있었지, 하고. 그 회지 만들 때 원고 모자라서 고생했잖아요. 기억나죠? 그래서 언니가 나한테 그

paid for the reviews. Not that the money's important. It's a small amount, anyway. Really nothing. I
also get invited to their events, but I seldom go. I
just show myself through my writing. I think writers
should exist through their writing. It won't do to
depend on those kinds of events all the time.

Anyway, I owe it all to you. I'm not good at writing novels, but I've grown into the habit of writing
down my ideas about every book I've read. I've
been writing them down in the pocketbook you
gave me. You advised me to leave everything in
writing, no matter what. That's why I set up that
blog and began posting my reviews. Honest to
God, I owe it to you. It's my review of your third
book that made all this happen. I was even awarded a prize with it at some book-review competi-
tion. Come to think of it, my blog began to gain
popularity around that time. Every now and then I
read the review again, and I still like it very much.

I've been closely following your work. Reading all
of your novels. Not only novels. Interview articles
and critiques as well. I even know what you've said
at which lecture. Moreover, I know your taste, personality, and professional background. As you said
yourself, it's because I know you so well that I was

얘기 써보라고 해서 쓴 건데. 물론 그때 언니가 손 좀 봐주긴 했지. 글 다 다듬어주고. 그래서 그런가, 비교해놓은 거 보니까 어떤 문장은 토씨 하나 안 틀리고 똑같더라? 혹시 그 회지에 있는 글 그대로 옮긴 거 아니에요? 물론 그럴 리는 없겠지.

제가요? 제가 왜요? 제가 올린 거 아니에요.

제가 왜 그런 일을 하겠어요?

그거 자유게시판에 올라온 글이에요. 아무나 다 들어와서 올려요. 사람들 하도 많이 오고 그러니까 댓글로만 안 돼서, 자유롭게 리뷰들 올리라고 방명록 개조해서 만든 거야. 그런데 그걸 제가 썼다고 생각하시면 안 되죠. 제가 그랬으면 그냥 책 읽어주는 여자 이름으로 올리죠. 왜 자유게시판으로 갔겠어요. 혹시 그 사람 누군지 알려달라고 연락하신 거예요? 가만있어보자, 그걸 어떻게 알아낼 수 있을까? 일단 IP주소를 알아내야 하는데…… 아니라니까요. 물론 그 얘긴 언니랑 나랑만 아는 거니까 그렇게 생각했을 수도 있겠다. 하지만 그 회지를 본 사람이 어디 저뿐이겠어요? 전교생이 다보는 건데. 어디 우리 학교뿐인가? 전국 대학에 다 돌렸

72

able to write a good review of your work. You once told me that once I have a good grasp of my subject, I'll be able to produce good work. Perhaps, there's an extra sense of genuineness in that review, since I know you well, then? Readers like the genuineness in that review. I think I realized at the time how important authenticity was. You always emphasized authenticity, remember? At the time, I couldn't understand what you meant by that. It finally dawned on me when I was writing the reviews of your novels.

It's more exciting than writing fiction. I've realized for the first time how much fun it is to live your life doing what you really want to do. Now that I've found what I really enjoy doing, I'm ready to clench my teeth and work away for another ten years.

Why aren't you eating? That's all you're eating today? You don't eat much, do you? That's probably how you lost so much weight. You look about ten kilograms lighter than you used to be. No, more than ten, I guess. Anyway, you look perfect as you are now. Is it because you've never had a child? Your figure's just like an unmarried woman. Ah, my mistake. You are indeed an unmarried woman. Of

잖아. 그 많은 사람들 중에 하나겠지. 그 많은 사람들 중에 언니 책 읽은 사람이 어디 한두 사람이겠어? 인기 작간데?

그런데 왜 꼭 저라고만 생각하세요?

언니도 참.

누가 갖고 있다가 어디서 본 거 같아서 찾아봤나 보지. 그 오래전 회지가 다 남아 있고. 참 놀라운 일이야. 그리고 뭐 없는 얘기 지어낸 건 아니더만. 거기 날짜도 명확히 쓰여 있고, 그러니 언니 소설보다 먼저 쓰인 것도 확실하고. 그것 땜에 문제가 되었어요? 하긴 그랬겠네. 겨우 학교 회지에 실린 학생 글 베껴 쓴 셈이 되었으니. 왜 아니겠어요? 블로그가 파워가 좀 있다 보니 그만큼 파급력도 있었나 보다. 삭제할걸 그랬네.

나는 그냥 블로그에다 재미로 올려본 건데.

네? 지금 내가 올렸다고 그랬다구요? 제가 언제요?

내가 재미로 올렸다고? 언제요?

아니에요. 잘못 들으신 거예요. 제가 쓴 게 아니라니까 그러시네요. 그게 다 언니가 신경이 예민해져서 그래. 제 추억을 소설로 쓴 게 미안해서 자꾸 그렇게 생각

course, you are, since you've never been married.

Now, I'd like a smoke. How about you? You've quit smoking? Oh my, you've quit. I've tried, but never succeeded. Except, just for one year when I was pregnant. During that time, I didn't even have to try. It was effortless.

Sister, you know what? I think I learned how to smoke from you. Yes, I'm sure. You taught me. I'm telling you. When I was just pretending to puff away, you told me not to smoke at all if I was going to continue to smoke like that. You said it was waste of cigarettes. Then, you taught me. I still remember the look on your face. Listen, and you're sure to remember.

Now, here's one naughty little kid. A naughty, demanding little troublemaker. He flops down on the floor and starts crying for cookies. I'm gonna throw a scare into this rotten little kid. So, you make a hissing sound by sucking in the air between your teeth. "*Hiss*! Now stand up right now or you'll get a smack!"

Now, apply that to smoking.—*Hiss* while inhaling and exhaling. *Hoooh*. Again, *Hiss* and *Hoooh*. You remember now, right? I felt dizzy as if I really had smacked somebody.

하시나 본데. 너무 신경 쓰지 마세요. 언니가 그 글을 베껴 쓴 것두 아니구. 나한테 들은 얘기 소설로 쓴 건데. 언니가 진정성 이런 거에 너무 집착하다 보니까, 내가 원망하고 있다고 생각해서, 그렇게 들린 거야. 그럴 필요 없어요. 사람이 적당히 타협할 줄도 알아야지. 그러다가 언니만 다쳐요. 물론 언니가 그거 쓰겠다고 나한테 허락을 받은 건 아니지만. 내 추억을 누구도 쓰면 안 된다고 상표등록 해놓은 것도 아니고. 내가 소유권 주장하겠다고 나설 사람도 아니고. 그런데 뭐가 걱정이에요. 그냥 유명세 치른다 생각하세요. 언니가 잘못 들은 거예요. 난 그렇게 말한 적 없어요.

　저, 소설 쓰냐고요? 소설을요? 에이 저 일찌감치 포기했어요. 잠깐, 그때 잠깐 써보려고 했죠. 그냥 언니 멋있어 보여서. 딱 한 편, 따라 해본 거죠. 그때 언니도 읽어 보셨잖아요. 제가 그거 보여드렸더니 언니가 그랬잖아요. 아줌마 글쓰기 하지 말라고. 문화센터 글쓰기 경멸한다고. 그래서 포기했어요. 아줌마가 쓸 수 있는 게 아줌마 글인데, 아줌마 글쓰기를 하지 말라고 하시니까. 어쩔 수 있나요? 쓰지 말아야지. 아줌마가 다시 처녀로

You made it so easy to learn. Making things easy for others to understand, that's also a talent, right? I still imagine giving some rotten little punk a smack on the back whenever I smoke.

Hiss. I smoked a lot by myself in the office of the Student Association after you graduated. *Hoooh.* The situation at school had gotten really bad by the time I graduated. People treated us leaders of the Student Association like invalids. It's just like how people treat smokers these days. "Why d'you keep smoking that unhealthy thing? You're hurting other people, too. Why don't you make yourself scarce and smoke over there, far away from the rest of us?"

Hiss. Things were really nice when you and I were at school together. We were always considerate of others. We knew when to feel sorry and when to feel obliged. We were grateful to those who took the lead to represent the interests of the rest of us. By the way, this restaurant isn't bad at all, allowing us to smoke. *Hoooh.* You enjoyed all those good years and got me on the last wagon before you ran off. After you betrayed me, you turned yourself into a writer and my plans went awry. Well, in fact, there's nothing particularly awry

돌아갈 수 있는 것도 아니고. 소설은 언니 같은 사람이 쓰는 거지. 나 같은 사람은 안 돼요.

그런데 최근에 학교 가보셨어요? 학교 진짜 많이 변했더라? 어디가 어딘지 도통 모르겠던걸? 전철역에서 학교로 바로 들어가는 출구도 생겼어요. 가보셨어요? 안 가보셨나 보네. 총여학생회실도 많이 변했더라구요.

그리고 나…… 언니네 집에 간 적 있어요. 언니는 모르겠지만.

그게 언제더라? 녹번동 그 집. 전복 한 바구니 들고. 왜 얘기 안 했냐고요? 얘기할 상황이 아니었지. 맞아요. 그럴 상황이 아니었어.

그게 그러니까 전복 때문에. 전복이요. 어느 날 신랑 거래처에서 전복을 선물 보내온 거야. 근데 그게 큼직 큼직한 게 꽤 먹잘 것이 있겠더라고. 너무 많기도 하고 언니 생각도 나고. 그래서 전화를 했지. 전복 얘기는 안 하구 그냥 언니네 집에 놀러 가면 안 되겠냐고. 서재 구경하고 싶다고. 그랬더니 언니가 마감 중이라 안 되겠다는 거야. 밥 먹을 시간도 없이 바쁘다고. 그래 알겠다고 했지. 가만 생각하니 너무 안쓰럽잖아. 소설이 뭐라

with my life right now.

If you say it isn't a betrayal, then so be it. I don't think you betrayed me, either. It's just other people who interpreted my situation that way at the time. They said they were sorry to see me betrayed by a senior whom I'd always loyally followed. They called me your follower. When that follower got betrayed, she was nothing but a kite with its string cut off. No. Worse than that. I was just holding onto the string after the kite cut itself free. Oh, I was such a fool. But that was a long time ago. I've forgotten all about it.

Hiss. By the way, do you still drink with a chop-stick stuck in your hair? Now, that's just a story of our youth now, isn't it? *Hoooh.* When I think of you every now and then, I like to twist my hair up with a chopstick and have a drink. Then, the liquor tastes so good. I wonder why. It's just a chopstick in my hair. A few times, I told the juniors the flag story. None of them properly understood it. They all stared at me as if to say, "What the heck are you talking about?" In fact, how can young people these days fully grasp that phrase, "grace period"? When I imitated you, do you know what they said? They said I was a giant phony. They asked what on

고 밥도 못 먹고 써? 그래서 일단 싸 들고 집을 나섰어. 전복만 얼른 전해주고 오려구. 괜찮으면 조용히 전복죽이나 끓여줄까 하고. 그런데 막상 언니 집 앞에 도착하니까 괜한 방해가 되려나 걱정이 되더라구. 원래 우리, 글 쓰는 사람들, 중간에 흐름이 흐트러지면 신경질 나잖아요. 내가 잘 알지. 어쩌나 싶어서 그냥 차 안에 앉아 있는데, 언니가 딱 오는 거야. 양손에 뭐 잔뜩 사가지고. 어떤 머리 허연 남자 팔짱을 끼고서.

사이가 좋아 보이더라? 밥 먹을 시간도 없다는 사람이?

기분 참 이상하더라. 이게 뭔가 싶고. 아무튼 그래서 그냥 집으로 왔어요. 대신 신랑이랑 둘이 앉아서 전복구이에다 맥주 한잔했지. 그런데 이 사람이 분위기 파악도 못 하고 언니 소설 칭찬을 막 하는 거야. 내가 읽어보라고 줬었거든. 뭐 소름이 돋을 정도로 좋았다나. 그런 소설 본 적이 없다면서. 아주 침이 튀어. 난 기분 나빠 죽겠는데. 그런데 또 뜬금없이 이러는 거야.

늙으면 거기 털도 하얘지나 봐?

그게 뭔소리야? 그랬더니. 왜 언니 소설에서 어떤 늙

earth I meant by "either I want to be *soju* or *soju* wants to be me." To borrow their jargon, I was "full of BS" Your university years were a good time. You had a junior like me who understood the meaning of the chopstick.

What's this? You've found it in my blog? Have I read it? Well, let me see. Ah... Yes, I think I've read it. That's right. I've read it. It compares your writing and my writing in that bulletin. I myself was very surprised to find it on the blog. It reminded me of the old days. When we were making that bulletin together, we had such a hard time because we didn't have enough manuscripts. Remember? So, you asked me to try writing a story. Of course, you proofread it for me, touching up here and there. I wonder if that's why. Now, when I compare the two, some sentences are even exactly the same. Have you, by any chance, copied my story from the bulletin? Of course, not. You couldn't have done that.

Me? Why would I? No, I didn't post it.

Why would I do a thing like that?

It was on the message board. Anybody can visit the site and post anything on the message board.

은 남자가 자기 거기 들여다보면서 새치 뽑는 장면이 나오잖아요? 그 얘기하는 거였더라구. 진짜 재밌었다구. 나는 재미도 없더만. 어쨌든 마침 맥주도 떨어지고 그래서 일어나 부엌으로 가려는데, 신랑이 허리를 확 끌어안으면서 나한테 물어. 아주 끈적한 목소리로.

그런데 그 언니작가는 그걸 어떻게 알았을까? 늙으면 거기 털도 하얘지는 거. 늙은이랑 자봤나? 아니면 어떻게 알았겠어? 젊은 여자가. 여류작가들은 다 그러고 사나 보지? 거기 새치도 서로 뽑아주고 그러나? 여보, 나도 한번 봐줘. 거기 털 하얘졌나 안 하얘졌나.

이러면서 막 웃어. 드럽고 불쾌한 기분이 드는데, 이게 또 아귀가 맞는 것두 같구, 아닌 것두 같구. 아무튼 그날 우리 신랑 진짜 끝내줬지. 전복 때문인지 뭐 때문인지, 밤새도록 아주우! 어머나 나 좀 봐. 결혼도 안 한 언니한테 이게 무슨 짓이야. 그렇게 인상 쓸 거 없어요. 아줌마들이 원래 이렇게 창피한 걸 모른다니까. 사우나가 봐요. 아줌마들 수건 둘러쓰고 벌거벗고 앉아서 이런 얘기 막 해. 땀 줄줄 흘리면서.

사람들은 소설과 현실을 구분을 못 해서 문제야. 소설

So many people visit my blog, so I can't handle the volume with the ripples alone. So, I remodeled the guest book to create a site so people can freely post their reviews. So, it doesn't make sense for you to think that I wrote that. I would have posted it on my own blog, "The Woman Who Reads for You." Why would I want to use the message board? Do you want to know who'd posted that review? Is that why you contacted me? Let's see. How can I find that person? First, I need the IP address... I swear, it's not me. You're singling me out because you think you and I are the only ones who know what happened at that time. But, we weren't that bulletin's only readers. The whole university read it. And it wasn't just our university, too. We distributed copies to every university across the country, too, remember? It's probably one of the old readers of the bulletin. Of all that bulletin's readers, quite a few probably read your book as well. You're a popular writer after all.

So why do you think it has to be me?

Come on, Sister.

Someone may have kept an old copy of the bulletin, and your story may have reminded that person of that story from that bulletin, and that person

가가 어떻게 경험한 것만 쓰겠어요? 그죠? 꼭 묻는 사람들 있어. 이거 직접 경험해보셨어요? 어떻게 이렇게 생생하게 쓸 수가 있죠? 참 바보들이라니까. 언니는 정말 그런 이상한 질문 많이 받았을 거 같아. 그런 거 일일이 응대하지 마세요. 괜히 언니 맘만 상하지. 나도 그날 신랑한테 엄청 뭐라 그랬다니까? 우리 신랑이 공대 출신이라 뭘 좀 몰라서 그래요. 신랑 대신 내가 사과할게.

이건 뭐예요? 블로그 글이요? 뭘 보라구요? 예, 봤어요. 읽어보라구요? 네, 읽었어요. 소리내서요? 초등학생도 아니구. 이걸 왜, 읽어요? 지금요? 그럼 어디 한번 읽어볼까요?

당신은 내게 깃발을 꽂으라고 하셨죠. 당신 깃발을 따라갔죠. 뭔가 나올 줄 알았죠. 그건 내 깃발이 아니었죠.

이 글을 제가 왜 읽어야 해요? 계속이요? 왜요? 읽어보라니까 읽기는 읽겠지만……

깃발을 뽑아 던졌지요. 깃발은 창이 되고 활이 되었지요. 사슴의 머리에. 곰의 심장에. 깃발은 나의 활 깃발은

may have looked it up. I just can't believe that old bulletin is still around somewhere. Isn't it amazing?

Although, to be fair, there's nothing actually false that anyone wrote in that review. The bulletin's clearly dated, too. Which proves it was written before your novel. Is there a problem because of that review? It's possible, I guess. Because it amounts to the fact that you copied a student's story from just some lowly school bulletin. So, it's only natural. Since my blog's rather powerful, I guess it can have that sort of ripple effect. I should have erased the review.

I just posted it on my blog for fun.

What? I just said I posted it? When did I say that?

I said that I did it for fun? When?

No. You must have heard me wrong. I'm telling you, I didn't write that review. You've become much too sensitive. Probably because you feel sorry that you used my childhood memory in your novel. But, don't worry about it. It's not like you copied it from anther printed source. You heard my story and put it in your novel. That's all. You're much too obsessed with things like authenticity so you believe that I must hold some sort of grudge against you. That's what made you hear me wrong.

나의 창. 당신의 깃발을 버리고 내 깃발을 꽂았어요. 사냥꾼이 되고 싶어요. 당신은 당신의 깃발. 나는 나의 깃발. 깃발을 꽂으세요. 그리고 펄럭이세요. 하늘 높이 하늘 높이. 펄럭이세요. 내 깃발은 당신의 심장을 향해 있어요.

제가 쓴 거냐고요? 음…… 그런가 보네요. 제가 쓴 거라고 쓰여 있는 거 보니. 이건 제가 쓴 글이 맞네요. 맞아요. 블로그 대문에 붙여놨던 글인 거 같네? 언니의 젓가락 깃발을 좀 변형해봤어요. 그런데 왜요? 언니 생각을 훔쳐 써서요? 기분 나쁘셨어요? 하지만 이 깃발은 언니 깃발하고는 완전 다른 거잖아요? 언니 젓가락은 십 년 인생 유예 기간에 관한 거구. 내 젓가락은 활에 관한 거예요. 활. 이건 훔쳐 쓴 게 아니라 발전한 거죠. 이 글 멋지지 않아요? 운율을 맞추느라 얼마나 힘들었는데.

당신,이요? 혹시 그 당신이 언니라고 생각하시는 건 아니죠? 소설가가 그런 질문을 하시면 안 되죠. 여기서 당신이 꼭 특정인물을 지칭하는 건 아니지. 그건 소설에서 그린 이야기를 직접 경험했냐고 물어보는 거하고 똑같은 거잖아. 잘 아시는 양반이 왜 그러세요. 언니한

No need to think that way. People need to learn to compromise to a certain degree. Otherwise, you'll only hurt yourself. Of course, you didn't get my permission to use that story in your novel. But, my memories aren't copyrighted, either. Moreover, I'm not the sort to come forward to claim my property rights. So, what's there to worry about? Just think of it as the price of fame. No. You must have heard me wrong. I never said that.

Me? Write novels? Are you asking if I write novels? No. I gave up on that early on. Wait a minute, I briefly tried to, as a matter of fact. Simply because you looked so cool. So, I just wrote one story, trying to imitate you. Didn't you also read it then, too? When I showed it to you, you told me I should stop writing like a housewife. You said you despised the type of writing they teach at cultural education centers. So, I gave it up. As a housewife, I couldn't help writing like a housewife. But then you told me not to write like a housewife. What was I supposed to do? So, I quit. There's no going back in time to my maiden days. Fiction writing belongs to people like you, Sister. Not to people like myself.

By the way, have you been to our university lately? Wow, so much has changed there. I couldn't

테서 깃발을 가져온 건 좀 미안하게 되었어요. 하지만 언니도 내 거 가져가셨잖아요.

내 닭 모가지.

그거 내 거 맞잖아요? 그래서 제가 뭐라 한 적이 있나요? 저 그런 사람 아니잖아요. 그냥 닭 모가지 받고 깃발 주셨다고 생각하세요. 고물상처럼. 언니는 부러진 닭 모가지 받고. 나는 뻥튀기 받고. 언니는 닭 모가지 받아서 소설 쓰고. 나는 뻥튀기 받아서 손가락에 끼고 놀고. 뻥튀기. 뻥튀기.

또 있어요? 지금 거기 가지고 계신 거 다 제 블로그에서 인쇄해 오신 거예요? 언니 내 블로그 탐구하셨나 보다. 일개 블로거의 글을 뭐 그렇게 열심히 따라 읽으세요? 부끄럽게. 글쎄 이건 어디 썼던 글이더라? 이건 내가 쓴 게 아닌 거 같은데? 댓글로 달렸던 건가?

항상 추종자들을 조심하세요. 추종자들이 추격에 나서면 진짜 무서운 사냥꾼이 되는 법이거든요. 왜냐, 너무 잘 아니까. 그럼 추종자가 무서운 사냥꾼이 되지 않게 하려면 어떻게 해야 할까요? 추종이 아니라 함께 가고 있다고 믿게 해줘야 한답니다. 가끔씩 자리를 내주기

even find my way around the campus. They built a new exit in the subway station that leads directly to the campus. Have you ever been there? I guess not. The office of the General Women Students Association's also changed a lot.

And I... I've been to your house. You wouldn't know, of course.

When? I mean that house in Nokbon-dong. I went there to give you a basketful of abalones. Why didn't I tell you at the time? The situation was rather unfavorable. Yes. It wasn't the right time and place to tell you.

It was all because of those abalones. Yes, abalo-nes. One day, a client of my husband's sent some abalones to us. The abalones were so big and looked delicious. There were so many of them, and I thought of you and called you. I didn't tell you about the abalones over the phone; I just asked if I could visit your home. I told you I wanted to see your study. You said you were so busy finishing up a work that you didn't even have time to eat. So, I said I understood. Then, I felt sorry for you. Is writing novels so great that it's worth skipping meals over it? I just left home with the bundle of abalones in my hand. I thought I'd just hand them

도 하세요. 정 자리를 내주기 싫으면, 그냥 엉덩이를 살짝 들었다 내리는 시늉이라도 해주세요. 명심하세요. 추종자들을 조심하라. 추종자들은 잠재적인 사냥꾼이다.

글쎄? 이건 잘 기억이 안 나네? 명심하라, 추종자들을 조심하라. 글쎄요. 잘 모르겠어요. 댓글인 게 분명해요. 엉덩이를 살짝 들었다 내리는 시늉이라도 해라. 댓글이네요. 누가 단 댓글인지는 모르겠지만 참 잘 썼네. 추종자들을 조심하라. 당연한 말씀. 추종자가 사냥꾼이 되는 순간. 무서운 거지. 어쩌면 이렇게 다 맞는 말일까?

그런데, 언니, 제가 꿈 얘기 하나 해드릴까요? 오랜만에 언니 만난다니까 어제 꿈에 언니가 나왔지 뭐야. 문학 하는 사람들이랑 무슨 공연장 같은 데 간 거야. 나무들이 둘러쳐져 있는 거 보면 산속인 것도 같구 해변인 것두 같구. 암튼 한판 축제가 벌어졌어. 공연도 하고 춤도 추고 낭독도 하고. 다들 즐거워 보이더라? 거기 한가운데 언니가 서 있는 거야. 꽃다발도 막 받구. 언니 무슨 상 같은 거 받을 건가 봐요? 언니도 이제 잘 팔리는 작가 말고 문학적으로도 인정받는 작가가 되셔야죠. 그죠? 암튼 나도 덩달아 좋은 구경하고 왔네? 꿈속인데도 진

over and then come back home. If it was all right with you, I was gonna make some abalone porridge for you. But when I stood in front of your house, I hesitated for fear of getting in the way of your work. You know how we writers hate it when the train of our thought gets disturbed in the middle. I know it well enough. I didn't know what to do, so I was just sitting in my car. Then you appeared with all those shopping bags in both of your hands. Arm in arm with that grey-haired man.

The two of you looked intimate. The woman who didn't even have time to eat?

I didn't even know what to feel. What's this? I thought. So, I just came back home. And had grilled abalones and beer with my husband. But then, this husband of mine didn't grasp the mood I was in and praised your novel to the skies. I'd given it to him to read a little while ago. Well, according to him, it was so good that he'd gotten goose bumps all over. He said he'd never read anything so good in his life. His praise went on and on, while I was just sat there, feeling awful. Then out of nowhere, he said:

I wonder if our you-know-where body hair also turns white?

짜 신나더라. 내가 상 받는 것처럼. 이런 거 태몽이라고 하나? 태몽도 누가 대신 꿔주고 그런다던데. 언니 좋은 일 생기면 내 꿈 덕분이라고 생각해줘요, 네?

어쨌거나 언니는 제 인생에서 정말 중요한 분이세요. 언니 덕분에 제가 있을 수 있었어요. 그야말로 나의 깃발, 이시죠. 정말이에요. 늘 고마워하고 있어요. 그러니까 언니, 제 부탁 들어주실 거죠? 작가와의 만남. 꼭 와주셔야 해요. 제가 차 가지고 모시러 갈게요. 와주세요. 와주실 거죠? 와주실 거라고 믿어요. 이번엔 제 믿음을 배신하지 마세요. 제가 언제 뭐 부탁한 적 없잖아요. 제가 부탁할 때 들으세요. 네?

『엄마도 아시다시피』, 문학과지성사, 2013

What're you talking about? I asked.

In fact, my husband was talking about the scene in your novel where an old man looks into his groin and pulls out all white hairs. He was talking about the scene. He said it was really interesting. Not really interesting to me, though. Anyhow, I noticed our beer bottles were empty. So, I was getting up to get some more from the kitchen when my hubby suddenly hugged my waist tight and, in a very greasy voice, asked:

By the way, how did your writer sister know about that? You know, the fact that your hair down there also turns white as you grow older? Has she ever slept with an old man? Otherwise, how would she know about something like that? She's a young woman, you know. Perhaps, all the women writers live like that? They and their partners help each other remove white hairs from down there? Honey, will you please check mine? See if there's any white hairs there.

Then, he burst into laughter. I felt lousy, so unpleasant. But then, I wasn't quite sure if what he'd said made sense or not. Anyway, that night, my hubby was superb. It may have been the abalones, or something else. My God—all night long.

Whoops! What on earth am I doing? What am I saying to an unmarried woman? Don't make a face like that. Housewives are notorious for their lack of shame. Go to a sauna and see for yourself. Housewives, stark naked except for a towel on their head, sit together and talk about things like this with no qualms whatsoever. Sweating profusely.

The problem is that people can't tell fiction from reality. How can a writer write only about the things she's experienced firsthand? Don't you agree? There's always those who ask: "Is this your personal experience? How do you describe it so vividly?" So foolish! You must have gotten so many silly questions like that. Don't even bother to respond to that kind of questions. It'll only make you feel bad. I also lashed out at my husband that day. His background is in engineering, so he knows virtually nothing outside the field. That's why he says things like that. I apologize on his behalf.

What is it this time? A blog entry? I'm supposed to look where? Yes, I see it. You want me to read it? Yes, I've read. Out loud? I'm not an elementary school kid. Why should I read it out loud? Now? Okay then, I'll read it.

You told me to raise the flag. I followed your flag.

I believed I would get somewhere. But it wasn't my kind of flag.

Why should I read this? Continue? Why? Okay, I'll keep reading since you ask me...

I pulled out the flag and threw it. That flag turned into spears and arrows. One aimed at a deer's head. Another at a bear's heart. The flag is my arrow. The flag is my spear. I cast away your flag and raise my own. I want to be a hunter. You have your flag. I have mine. Raise your flag. And let it fly. High, high up in the sky. Let it unfurl. My flag is aimed at your heart.

Did I write it? Hmm... I guess so. Since my name's written right there. It's my writing. Yes, it is. It seems to be the one I've posted on my blog homepage. I've tweaked your flag story a little bit. Is there a problem? You think I've stolen your thoughts? So, you're offended? But, this flag story is completely different from yours, isn't it? Your chopstick story is about a decade-long grace period. My chopstick story is about a bow. A bow! This isn't stealing, but developing something further. Isn't the writing wonderful, though? I worked very hard to get the meter right.

You mean the "you" in this piece of writing? You

don't think that's you, do you? You, a writer, shouldn't ask that kind of question. The "you" here isn't necessarily any specific person. It's just like asking a writer if her story is from her actual experiences. You know better than that. I'm sorry that I took your idea about flags. But, you also took one of mine.

My idea of chicken necks.

That was my idea. Right? Have I ever complained to you about it? You know I'm not that kind of person. Just think of it as a trade, my chicken neck for your flag. Like at a secondhand store. You got a broken chicken neck and I got some popped rice. You used the chicken neck in your novel. I balanced the popped rice on my fingers and played with them. Pop-pop-pop.

There's more? All the printouts you have there are from my blog? You've really studied my blog. What's made you so interested in the writings of a mere blogger? You're making me blush. Well, where did I post this one? This doesn't sound like my writing. Is this one of the ripples?

Always be wary of your followers. They make formidable hunters once they're on your tail. How? They know you so well, that's how. What can you do to stop your followers from turning into fierce hunters? You've got to make them believe that they're not following you, but walking together with you side by side. You'll have to give up your seat to them every now and then. When you really don't want to give it up, you should at least make an effort to pretend to yield, just briefly lifting yourself up off your seat. Keep that in mind. Be wary of your followers. They're all potential hunters.

Well? I don't recall writing this one. Keep that in mind. Be wary of your followers. Well. I'm not sure. It must be one of the ripples. Pretend to yield by briefly lifting yourself up off your seat. That's definitely a ripple. Whoever wrote it, it's very good. Be wary of your followers. Of course! When the followers become hunters, they can be formidable. It makes so much sense, every word of it.

By the way, Sister. Let me tell you about my dream. You appeared in my dream last night. It's probably because I was thinking about our meeting today. You and I and some other writers were on our way to see a performance or something. There were trees surrounding the place; it seemed like maybe it was in a mountain or on a beach. Anyway, a feast was already going on when we arrived there. Some people were acting, some dancing, others reciting their works. People were having a wonderful time. You stood right in the middle of it all. You were receiving bouquet after bouquet. I think you were going to be awarded some kind of prize. I hope you go beyond being a bestselling author, and become a critically recognized one.

Anyway, I also had a good time in my dream. It was only a dream, but I was so happy nonetheless. It was as if I were the one receiving the award. Might this be one of those "precognitive dreams?" I heard that, in the case of dreams where someone's about to conceive, someone else might have a precognitive dream for the future mother. If something good happens to you, remember that you owe it to my dream. Would you, please?

No matter what, you're a truly important person in my life. Thanks to you, I've become what I am now. You're my flag, truly. I mean it. I'll always be grateful to you. So, Sister. You'll accept my invitation, won't you? To come to our Meet the Writer session? You must come, please. I'll come pick you up. Please, do come. You will come, won't you? I trust you'll come. Please, don't betray my trust this time. I've never asked you a favor until now. So, you'll do me a favor when I ask you. Please?

Translated by Jeon Miseli

해설

Afterword

모두가 모른 척하는, 누구나 아는 욕망

전소영 (문학평론가)

불과 십여 년 전의 일이었나 보다. 한국 문단이 천운영이라는 '무서운' 신예 소설가를 맞이하게 된 것은. 말 그대로 무서운 신인이었다. 첫 단편 「바늘」에서부터 이 작가는 그랬다. 저마다의 마음 깊숙이 잠복해 있는 관능, 공격성, 탐미의식에 관해 말하는 것을 도통 주저하지 않는 듯했다. 이후로도 그 거리낌 없는 이야기는 계속되었고 이 작가의 소설은 줄곧, 예외도 없이 우리 앞에 '떨림'으로 도착했다. 그 도착을 어떤 이들은 강렬하다고 했고, 다른 이들은 그로테스크 하다고도 했다.

다만 떨림이라는 것이 적어도 두 가지 상반된 성분을 지닌다는 것을 떠올릴 수 있었으면 좋겠다. 최초의 떨

Unacknowledged Desires

Jeon So-yeong (literary critic)

It was only ten-odd years ago when the Korean literary circles welcomed a "formidable" new writer named Cheon Un-yeong. In her first short story "Needle," Cheon seemed to have absolutely no scruples talking about the carnal desire, aggression, and aesthetic obsession hidden deep in the heart of every one of us. Her unreserved narrative style has since continued in her short stories and full-length novels that have always managed to reach us, indeed, managed to always leave us absolutely *trembling*.

Some might describe this trembling as intense and others as grotesque but here I would like to

림은 물론 두려움으로 느껴질 것이다. 위험이나 초조로 삶이 소스라치는 순간이 있다. 우리가 끝내 몰랐으면 했던 어떤 진실들에 닿을 때 그러한데, 천운영의 소설은 늘 진실에 가까워졌음을 알리는 경보(警報)처럼 울렸다. 그리고 이 진실이란 대체로 우리의 내밀한 욕망, 우리도 하나쯤 가슴팍에 숨겨두고 있지만 꺼내기 거북해하는 그런 것이었다. 그 꺼려지는 것을 아무렇게나 획 코앞에 내미는 소설들 앞에서 우리는 속수무책으로 일렁여야 했던 것이다.

그러나 떨림은 설렘과 그다지 다르지 않다는 사실도 잊지 않았으면 좋겠다. 이 작가가 내내 해왔던 작업, 누구도 차마 앞장서 말하려고 하지 않는 것에 대해 말하는 일은 어렵지만 옳고, 아름답다. 우리가 이 작가의 소설을 계속 따라 읽는 이유가 거기에 있을 것이다. 이제 다시 두려워하며 설레 하며 「젓가락여자」를 펼친다.

이 소설이 바드럽게 느껴질 수밖에 없었다면, 이곳이 또 하나의 욕망 전시장이기 때문이다. 전체 서사라야 익명의 파워 리뷰어인 여인이 자기가 속한 독서 토론회에, 과거 친한 선배였던 서진 작가를 초대하는 내용이 전부. 그러나 이 안에 작가는 누구나 가졌을 법한, 대개

point out that this exact condition consists of at least two quite different emotional components: fear and anticipation. Usually, fear tends to be the initial feeling of this trembling. There are revelatory moments in life when we are frightened or irritated by the hidden truths we would prefer to remain ignorant of to the end. Cheon's fiction, however, always reads as a loud and clear warning of the truths that sneak up on us closer than ever—the truths of the human desires that always remained present somewhere inside of us, no matter how reluctant we are to admit it. We cannot help being shaken to the bone reading Cheon's works whose works never fail to reveal those long-suppressed truths nonchalantly before our unsuspecting eyes.

On the other hand, it is also important to keep in mind that this sort of trembling is not so different from the thrill of anticipation. What Cheon has been doing all along is telling the truths that no one else has dared to confront openly. It's a difficult, and yet just and admirable task. This is probably why we continue reading Cheon's stories. Now, I feel like I am ready to read her short story "Chopstick Woman" once more, trembling with fear and anticipation.

는 비밀로 하고 싶어 할 다채로운 욕망들을 진열해놓았다. 정확히 말하면 욕망이 만들어지고 좌절되고 변질되는 과정을 꺼내놓았다.

먼저 소설을 가로지르는 가장 큰 욕망, 글쓰기 혹은 작가되기. 우리가 열망으로든 콤플렉스로든 한번쯤은 품어봄직한 것. 화자도 그랬다. 존경하는 선배를 좇아 소설을 써보려 했지만, 애 엄마가 되어서도 희망을 놓지 못하지만, 그것은 정작 선배의 냉혹한 진단에 의해 깨어진다. 반전은 그 선배 작가가 실은 화자의 이야기를 베껴 소설을 지어왔다는 사실이다. 여기 또 하나의 욕망, 지나치게 매혹적이라 종종 윤리를 넘어서는 훔치기의 욕망이 드러났다.

이 망연자실한 상황에, 한때 동경했던 소설가에게 복수하기 위해 화자가 리뷰어가 된다는 사실은 되새겨 음미해볼 만하다. 어쩌면 이 관계도가 작중에서 가장 빛나는 지점이 될 것이다. 소설 속 리뷰어는 소설가의 안티를 자청하지만, 그 자청이 전적으로 진담이 될 수 없다는 것을 우리는 안다. 리뷰어라는 존재가 그렇다. 일단은 팬이다. 소설을 깎아내리든 추켜세우든, 일단 그것을 면밀하게 촘촘하게 읽어내어야 하는 것이다. 더군

If this story makes the reader feel vulnerable, it is because it is yet another exhibition of the reality of our deepest human desires. The plot itself is quite simple: the narrator, an anonymous "power reviewer" invites So Jin, a writer and her once close college senior mate, to her reading club meet. Nevertheless, the story presents a variety of desires that we all are likely to possess and yet endeavor to keep hidden. In particular, "Chopstick Woman" seems to make special efforts to describe the process in which desires are generated, frustrated, and degenerated in the end.

The leitmotif of Cheon's story is the desire to tell stories, to be some form of writer at some point. At least once in our lifetime, we may also experience the same desire, whether it stems from passion or obsession. The narrator in this story is no exception. She strives to be a writer like her senior, her hope never fading even after she marries and becomes a mother. Her dreams, however, are dashed by a withering critique from none other than this So Jin who, in a sudden reversal, is revealed to be something of a plagiarist of the narrator's stories. Here is another type of desire, then, the desire to steal. The seductive power that often

다나 여인이 '파워 블로거'였으니 소설에 들인 그녀의 공을 짐작하고도 남겠다. 리뷰어와 소설가는 서로를 원수처럼 여기지만, 리뷰어는 소설을 미워하며 글을 쓴다. 소설가는 리뷰어의 이야기를 훔쳐 글을 쓴다. 이 비정한 욕망의 연쇄가 끝끝내 그들로 하여금 글을 쓰게 한다. 그 끝에 소설은 이렇게 말하는 것도 같다. 글쓰기란 그 자체로 욕망덩어리인 것이다.

꿈이 함부로 짓이겨지고 깨어졌을 때, 화자의 복수가 시작된다. 본래 극에서 극으로 치닫는 것은 쉬운 일이라 했다. 동경에의 열망이 똑같은 질량의 파괴에의 열망으로 바뀌었다 해도 될 것이다. 화자는 서진 작가의 비밀을 폭로하고, 때론 잔인하게 그것을 파고들며 복수를 시작한다. 그러면서 질투, 폭로, 위협, 냉소라는 욕망의 부산물들이 여기저기 고개를 내민다.

이것은 익숙한데다 얼마간은 뜨끔하다. 소설 속에 가로 놓인 모든 욕망들이 실은 나와 당신과 멀지 않은 것 같다. 정확히는 우리 모두의 마음 깊은 곳과 맞닿아 있다. 그걸 내내 상기시키려 화자, 그리고 작가는 독자를 거듭 향해 있다. 말을 걸고 묻고 되물으며 대답을 요청하는 서술 방식으로 우리를 찌른다. 그것은 이런 질문

forces people to cross their most cherished ethical boundaries.

At this point, it is crucial to consider the notion that the narrator has only become a reviewer to wreak her vengeance on the senior whom she once so admired. Perhaps, mapping this causal relation creates the tension at the height of this story. The reviewer in the story claims to be an anti-fan of the writer's. Nevertheless, we readers know that it cannot be wholly truthful, considering the very nature of reviewers. They are first and foremost fans of the writers they review. Whether they criticize or extol a work, they must read it first both meticulously and thoroughly. Judging by the fact that the reviewer in the story is a "power" blogger, we can easily imagine how much work she has put into reading a writer's works. The reviewer and the writer are at odds with each other. The reviewer writes about the writer's stories while hating them as the writer steals the reviewer's stories. The desires of the two are locked in a cruel chain of causality, ultimately compelling both to keep writing in a vicious cycle of sorts. Writing, "Chopstick Woman" seems to tell us, is a tangled web of desires.

When the narrator divulges that her dream has

이기도 하다. 나와 당신들이 다른가? 대답은 어디까지나 저마다의 몫일 것이다. 다만 마지막까지도 개과천선의 기미 없는 화자가 그저 미워 보이지만은 않았거나 그녀에 이입이 되지는 않았는가? 그렇다면 우리, 그녀와 다르지 않은 것이다.

been all but trampled and destroyed she confesses that it was at this point where she began to take her revenge. As one extreme often easily transmutes itself into another, the narrator's once extreme level of admiration turns into an extreme passion for destruction. The narrator reveals her former friend's secret as her first act of revenge, much to the chagrin and public embarrassment of the writer. And such by-products of her desire—jealousy, threats, and mockery—begin to rear their heads here.

These elements of human nature, all too familiar to us, can often sting. The desires displayed throughout Cheon's story are not too far from those of yours or mine. They arouse a response deep down in our hearts, reminding us of that resonance, the narrator, or the writer, and repeatedly asking the same question, "Are you different from me?" This question demands our answer. We may come up with different answers to this question, but, as a reader myself, I would like to ask a slightly different question: Do you find yourself unable to hate the narrator despite the fact that she shows no sign of penance till the very end? Or, do you empathize with the narrator? If the answer to either question is yes, we may not be quite so different from her "Chopstick Woman's" unnamed narrator.

비평의 목소리

Critical Acclaim

이 작가에게 삶은 스크린으로 편안하게 감상하거나 관조할 수 있는 대상이 아니다. 인터넷에 부단히 명멸하는 한갓 정보의 부나비일 수 없다. 삶은 결코 그런 것이 아니다. 영화의 한 장면이었으면 좋겠고, 꿈이었으면 좋겠지만, 결코 몽유록이 아닌 고통의 생생한 파노라마가 바로 삶이다. 아무리 세기가 바뀌고 세상이 변했다고 하더라도 여전히, 변함없이, 혹은 더욱이 가중되는 삶의 고통스러운 현장을, 천운영은 한시라도 외면하고 싶어 하지 않는다. 그렇다고 해서 남들도 다 짐작할 수 있는 고통의 현장, 그러니까 유형적이거나 전형적인 고통의 현장을 체험하고 싶어 하는 것 같지는 않

A Way to Give Shapes to Life: To this writer, life is not a distant object to appreciate or contemplate comfortably as if presented on movie screen, nor data perpetually flickering away on the Internet, nor our many dream sequences. Life is a long series of painful, real events. Though the world has changed over the centuries, there still remain the same or even more painful realities of life that Cheon Un-yeong never averts her eyes from. Nevertheless, the writer does not seem to focus on stereotypical sufferings. Instead, she seems determined to shed light on the painful events taking place in the inconspicuous, peripheral spheres of

다. 가능하면 다른 사람들의 눈길이 성긴 외진 곳에서, 변두리에서 벌어지는 고통스런 사건들에 새로운 성찰의 빛을 사하고 싶어 한다. 고통의 현장을 탐사하는 성찰의 빛이 강렬할수록 비극적 세계관은 깊어진다.

우찬제

천운영 소설의 유전자는 90년대 이래 여성소설의 성과와 한국소설의 본류 중 하나인 남성적 리얼리즘의 공력이 결합된 곳에서 생겨났다고 해야 한다. 이를테면 오정희와 전경린의 어떤 것이 황석영과 김소진의 어떤 것과 만나 일으킨 화학작용이라 해도 좋다. 그 화학작용의 결과물은 평단의 대대적인 환영을 받았다. 페미니즘은 그녀의 소설에서 90년대 여성소설의 여성상을 넘어서는 가능성을 보았고, 리얼리즘은 그녀의 소설에서 리얼리즘의 갱신을 위한 단초를 보았다.

신형철

작가 천운영은 자신의 아비들과의 관계를 단절하고 스스로의 기원을 형성해가는, 일종의 사생아에 가까운 작가이다. 하지만 그 형식에 관해 말하자면 그의 소설

society. The more intense the light, the more insightful her tragic view of the world.

U Chan-je

The genetic make-up of Cheon Un-yeong's fiction was born where the successful feminist novels of the 1990s and the efforts of masculine realism, one of the main currents of Korean fiction, first met. For example, when the elements of Oh Jung-hee and Jeon Kyong-rin met with many of the elements of Hwang Sok-yong and Kim So-jin, a sort of chemical action occurred. The results of this chemical action have been greatly welcomed by the critics. Feminism saw something in Cheon's fiction that could enable her work to go beyond the images of women in 1990s feminist fiction even while realism witnessed its first steps towards its ultimate renovation.

Shin Hyeong-cheol

Cheon Un-yeong is something of an illegitimate child, severing her ties with her father while creating an origin of her own. When it comes to her fiction's form, however, her works faithfully and insistently succeed in the grammar of the existing short

은 기존의 단편소설의 문법을 충실하고도 완미하게 계승한다. 천운영은 묘사와 서사, 부분과 전체의 조화라는 단편소설의 철칙을 충실하게 따를 뿐만 아니라 하나의 절정을 향해 아주 모범적인 방식으로 사건을 배열해 나간다. 그리고 이어지는 절정 끝의 결말들. 천운영의 소설은 이렇게 낯설고 괴상망측한 내용을 완미한 소설적 형식에 적절하게 녹여내면서 한국소설의 새로운 영역을 개척해왔다.

류보선

한국 문학에 독특한 여성 캐릭터의 이미지를 새겨 넣으면서 여성성의 문학적 의미를 갱신한 작가 천운영. 작가는 1990년대 여성 소설의 성취를 껴안고 상투적인 여성 이미지를 창조적으로 넘어설 수 있는 소설적 가능성을 시험해왔다. 이런 이유로 독자들은 천운영 소설이 선보인 작가적 개성의 매력을 넘어, 작가의 '미래' 작업에 더욱 주목하지 않을 수 없게 된다.

이광호

그의 묘사는 대상에 밀착하여 느린 속도로 촬영하는

story. The ironbound laws of short story writing—the harmony between description and narration and between the parts and the whole—her work strictly observes. Furthermore, Cheon's plot structure closely follows the prototypical procession towards climax and denouement. By skillfully melding and shaping her grossly unfamiliar and grotesque contents into the rigid novelistic form, Cheon's works have been opening up new horizons for Korean fiction.

Ryu Bo-seon

By inscribing unique female characters in the world of Korean literature Cheon Un-yeong has given a new literary meaning to femininity. Working from the foundation of the successful feminist novels of the 1990s, Cheon experiments with the novelistic possibilities of creatively transcending the stereotypical images of women. For this reason, the reader cannot but try to see beyond her fascinating authorial personality and pay closer attention to the task she will take on in the future.

Lee Kwang-ho

Her depictions of characters and events give the

카메라의 눈을 통해 바라보는 듯한 인상을 주기도 하고, 대상을 굴절시키는 특정한 주관적인 시각을 계속 의식하게 만들기도 한다. 후자는 주로 대상에 중첩된 강렬한 이미지에서 두드러지지만, 대상을 바라보는 각도 자체에서 드러나기도 한다. 어떤 관찰이든 주관성에서 벗어날 수는 없는 것이겠지만, 천운영의 묘사는 객관성과 주관성을 각각 극대화하면서 결합하는 듯한 느낌을 준다. 여기에는 작품의 의미체계를 세목에까지 단단하게 관철해나가고자 하는 작가적 의지가 배어 있으며, 이는 전복과 해체의 시도와도 연계되어 있는 것으로 보인다.

김영희

reader an impression of seeing things through the lens of a slow-speed, close-up camera; they make us constantly conscious of a particular subjective perspective that refracts the object's image. The latter is marked mainly in the intense images superimposed on objects; but it is also revealed in the angle from which the object is viewed. Of course, no observation is free from the observer's subjectivity. Nonetheless, Cheon's literary depictions seem to maximize both objectivity and subjectivity, while trying to amalgamate the two. Here, we witness the writer's will to apply the semantic system of her fiction even to the minute details of her stories, which seem to be linked to her attempts to overturn and deconstruct it.

Kim Yeong-hui

천운영

　소설가 천운영은 1971년 서울에서 태어나 2000년 대략 서른 살쯤 작가의 길로 접어들었다. 처음엔 대학에서 신문방송학을 전공했고, 소설 공부를 하기 위해 다시 문예창작학과 학생이 되었다. 그러나 그녀는, 대부분의 작가 지망생처럼 열렬히 문학에 사로잡혔던 것은 아니었다고 했다. 문예창작학과 입학 후의 한동안은 고생의 연속이었다. 수업 시간에 모르는 작가의 이름을 너무 많이 들어서 공책에 그것을 빠짐없이 적어뒀다가, 강의가 끝나면 도서관으로 달려갔다고 한다. 그런 식으로 이 작가는 독서 경험을 쌓아올렸다. 대학생활은 물론 그녀에게 다행스러운 경험도 남겼다.

　노력의 시간을 거쳐 「바늘」로 이름을 알렸고 소설집 『바늘』(2001)과 『명랑』(2004)만으로 한국 문단의 문제 작가가 되었다. 그러니 조금쯤은 쉴 법도 한데 그녀의 소설쓰기는 쉼이 없었다. 장편소설 『잘 가라, 서커스』(2005)와 『생강』(2011), 소설집 『그녀의 눈물 사용법』(2008)과 『엄마도 아시다시피』(2013)가 그 성실함의 결

Cheon Un-yeong

Cheon Un-yeong was born in Seoul in 1971 and made her debut as a writer in 2000. In university, she first majored in mass communication and then in creative writing. At the beginning of her studies in the Department of Creative Writing, however, she had a hard time getting as passionately involved in literature as her fellow would-be writers. Unfamiliar with so many new writers, Cheon began the habit of writing them down in her notebook and rushing to the library immediately after the lectures, this eventually becoming the base of her reading experience.

Her unabating creative efforts finally came to fruition when she made a name for herself with "Needle." With the collections of short stories *Needle* and *Cheerfulness* alone, she began to create a sensation in Korean literary circles. Since her initial success, she has never relaxed her efforts. The full-length novels, *Farewell Circus* and *Ginger*, and her collections of short stories, *Her Use of Tears* and *As Mom Also Knows,* are the proof of her diligence

실이다.

『바늘』에서는 강함과 약함, 아름다움과 추함을 찔렀고『명랑』에서는 삶과 죽음의 문제에 파고들었다. 낯설다, 칼날같다는 평가에서 조금 물러선 첫 작품이 조선족 동포들의 삶을 따뜻하게 감싼『잘 가라, 서커스』였다. 한결 부드럽게 읽힌다는 언급이, 상처와 눈물로 나아간『그녀의 눈물 사용법』으로도 이어졌다.

『생강』은 좀 다른 의미에서 화제가 되었다. 거기에서 작가는 고문기술자 이근안의 사건을 모티프로 다뤘다. 발품 팔아 소재를 모으고, 주변 관찰을 게을리하지 않는 그녀의 이른바 '취재적 글쓰기'가 빛을 발했다. 작가는 언젠가 이렇게 말하기도 했다. "소설을 쓰는 건 누군가를 관찰하는 거죠. 취재 없이는 인간에 대해 쓸 수 없어요. 화장을 안 하고, 속이지 않고, 아는 척하지 않고 싶어요. 그게 소설에 대한 변함없는 태도예요." 이런 언급을 덧붙여도 되겠다. "취재 다니면서 스스로 흥분되는 게 느껴져요. 제가 좀 즉물적이거든요. 직접 만진 것, 본 것, 느낀 것만 믿어요. 몸이 반응하는 게 제가 생각하는 것이죠. 몸의 언어여야 진짜 언어라고 생각해요. 중요한 건 '내가 쓴다'는 거죠. 내 몸이 접하는 세상, 내가

and devotion to her craft.

In *Needle*, she scrutinizes the contrasts between strength and weakness and beauty and ugliness while in *Cheerfulness*, she probes the themes of life and death. *Farewell Circus*, on the other hand, was her first work that helped relieve her from the critiques that deemed her works as unfamiliar or scathing. *Farewell Circus* depicted the life of the ethnic Koreans in China with pathos and compassion, making it easier to read for many critics. *Her Use of Tears*, likewise, dealt with pain and personal trauma and enjoyed similarly positive critical responses.

Ginger, meanwhile, received attention for a slightly different reason. The writer adopts the Torture Expert Lee Geun-an Incident as the motif for *Ginger*. Her endeavors in finding facts and her power of observation and "journalistic writing" shine through. On one occasion, the writer states, "Story-writing is observing someone. Without fact-finding efforts, I can't write about human beings. I don't want to put on makeup, I don't want to tell lies, and I don't want to pretend to be knowledgeable. That's my consistent attitude towards creative writing." On another occasion, Cheon also notes,

바라는 세상을 쓰는 거죠."

　삶의 전방위를 더듬는 취재원의 길을 거쳐 작가는 지금 『엄마도 아시다시피』를 통해 안쪽으로, 자기에게로, 엄마에게로 돌아왔다. 다음엔 그의 예각적인 시선이 또 어떤 생의 심부에 닿을지, 기대해봐도 좋을 것이다.

"While gathering facts, I can feel myself getting excited. I've a practical turn of mind. I believe only the things that I can touch, see, and feel first-hand. How my body reacts is what I think. As for me, this language of the body is the only authentic language. What's important is 'it's I who writes.' I'm writing about a world my body comes in contact with and a world that I wish to live in."

Cheon Un-yeong began her writer's life as a reporter probing life in all its aspects. She has since set out on an inward journey in *As Mom Also Knows* to reach her inner self and her mother. Now, I wonder what will be the next thing her keen eyes catch sight of in the depths of her life.

번역 **전미세리** Translated by Jeon Miseli

한국외국어대학교 동시통역대학원을 졸업한 후, 캐나다 브리티시컬럼비아 대학교 도서관학, 아시아학과 문학 석사, 동 대학 비교문학과 박사 학위를 취득하고 강사 및 아시아 도서관 사서로 근무했다. 한국국제교류재단 장학금을 지원받았고, 캐나다 연방정부 사회인문과학연구회의 연구비를 지원받았다. 오정희의 단편 「직녀」를 번역했으며 그 밖에 서평, 논문 등을 출판했다.

Jeon Miseli is graduate from the Graduate School of Simultaneous Interpretation, Hankuk University of Foreign Studies and received her M.L.S. (School of Library and Archival Science), M.A. (Dept. of Asian Studies) and Ph.D. (Programme of Comparative Literature) at the University of British Columbia, Canada. She taught as an instructor in the Dept. of Asian Studies and worked as a reference librarian at the Asian Library, UBC. She was awarded the Korea Foundation Scholarship for Graduate Students in 2000. Her publications include the translation "Weaver Woman"(*Acta Koreana*, Vol. 6, No. 2, July 2003) from the original short story "Chingnyeo"(1970) written by Oh Jung-hee.

감수 **전승희, 데이비드 윌리엄 홍**

Edited by Jeon Seung-hee and David William Hong

전승희는 서울대학교와 하버드대학교에서 영문학과 비교문학으로 박사 학위를 받았으며, 현재 하버드대학교 한국학 연구소의 연구원으로 재직하며 아시아 문예 계간지 《ASIA》 편집위원으로 활동 중이다. 현대 한국문학 및 세계문학을 다룬 논문을 다수 발표했으며, 바흐친의 『장편소설과 민중언어』, 제인 오스틴의 『오만과 편견』 등을 공역했다. 1988년 한국여성연구소의 창립과 《여성과 사회》의 창간에 참여했고, 2002년부터 보스턴 지역 피학대 여성을 위한 단체인 '트랜지션하우스' 운영에 참여해 왔다. 2006년 하버드대학교 한국학 연구소에서 '한국 현대사와 기억'을 주제로 한 워크숍을 주관했다.

Jeon Seung-hee is a member of the Editorial Board of *ASIA*, and a Fellow at the Korea Institute, Harvard University. She received a Ph.D. in English Literature from Seoul National University and a Ph.D. in Comparative Literature from Harvard University. She has presented and published numerous papers on modern Korean and world literature. She is also a co-translator of Mikhail Bakhtin's *Novel and the People's Culture* and Jane Austen's *Pride and Prejudice*. She is a founding member of the Korean Women's Studies Institute and of the biannual Women's Studies' journal *Women and Society* (1988), and she has been working at 'Transition House,' the first and oldest shelter for battered women in New England. She organized a workshop entitled "The Politics of Memory in Modern Korea" at the Korea Institute, Harvard University, in 2006. She also served as an advising committee member for the Asia-Africa Literature Festival in 2007 and for the POSCO Asian Literature Forum in 2008.

데이비드 윌리엄 홍은 미국 일리노이주 시카고에서 태어났다. 일리노이대학교에서 영문학을, 뉴욕대학교에서 영어교육을 공부했다. 지난 2년간 서울에 거주하면서 처음으로 한국인과 아시아계 미국인 문학에 깊이 몰두할 기회를 가졌다. 현재 뉴욕에서 거주하며 강의와 저술 활동을 한다.

David William Hong was born in 1986 in Chicago, Illinois. He studied English Literature at the University of Illinois and English Education at New York University. For the past two years, he lived in Seoul, South Korea, where he was able to immerse himself in Korean and Asian-American literature for the first time. Currently, he lives in New York City, teaching and writing.

바이링궐 에디션 한국 대표 소설 074
젓가락여자

2014년 6월 6일 초판 1쇄 인쇄 | 2014년 6월 13일 초판 1쇄 발행

지은이 천운영 | 옮긴이 전미세리 | 펴낸이 김재범
감수 전승희, 데이비드 윌리엄 홍 | 기획 정은경, 전성태, 이경재
편집 정수인, 이은혜 | 관리 박신영 | 디자인 이춘희
펴낸곳 (주)아시아 | 출판등록 2006년 1월 27일 제406-2006-000004호
주소 서울특별시 동작구 서달로 161-1(흑석동 100-16)
전화 02.821.5055 | 팩스 02.821.5057 | 홈페이지 www.bookasia.org
ISBN 979-11-5662-018-1 (set) | 979-11-5662-036-5 (04810)
값은 뒤표지에 있습니다.

Bi-lingual Edition Modern Korean Literature 074
Chopstick Woman

Written by Cheon Un-yeong I **Translated by** Jeon Miseli
Published by Asia Publishers I 161-1, Seodal-ro, Dongjak-gu, Seoul, Korea
Homepage Address www.bookasia.org I **Tel**. (822).821.5055 I **Fax**. (822).821.5057
First published in Korea by Asia Publishers 2014
ISBN 979-11-5662-018-1 (set) | 979-11-5662-036-5 (04810)

〈바이링궐 에디션 한국 대표 소설〉 작품 목록(1~60)

아시아는 지난 반세기 동안 한국에서 나온 가장 중요하고 첨예한 문제의식을 가진 작가들의 작품들을 선별하여 총 105권의 시리즈를 기획하였다. 하버드 한국학 연구원 및 세계 각국의 우수한 번역진들이 참여하여 외국인들이 읽어도 어색함이 느껴지지 않는 손색없는 번역으로 인정받았다. 이 시리즈는 세계인들에게 문학 한류의 지속적인 힘과 가능성을 입증하는 전집이 될 것이다.

바이링궐 에디션 한국 대표 소설 set 1

분단 Division

산업화 Industrialization

여성 Women

바이링궐 에디션 한국 대표 소설 set 2

자유 Liberty

바이링궐 에디션 한국 대표 소설 set 3

바이링궐 에디션 한국 대표 소설 set 4

디아스포라 Diaspora

가족 Family

유머 Humor